SEESAW SUNDAY

by LEON ARDEN

NOVELS

The Savage Place
Seesaw Sunday

PLAYS

This Way Lies Madness, That Way
Lies Newark (with Flip Schaffer)

Seesaw Sunday

Leon Arden

For Jay and Lois Seeman

ACKNOWLEDGMENTS

Lyrics from "What Is This Thing Called Love?" by Cole Porter. © 1929 by Harms, Inc. Used by permission of Music Publishers Holding Corp., New York, N.Y.

Lyrics from "Where Are You?" Lyrics by Harold Adamson, music by Jimmy McHugh. © 1936 by Universal Music Corporation, New York, N.Y. All rights throughout the world controlled by Leo Feist, Inc., New York, N.Y. Used by permission.

Lyrics from "This Love of Mine," Sol Parker, Henry Sanicola, Frank Sinatra. © 1941 by Embassy Music Corporation, 240 West 55th Street, New York, N.Y. 10019. Used by special permission.

Lyrics from "I Get Along Without You Very Well," by Hoagy Carmichael. © 1938 and 1939 by Famous Music Corporation, New York, N.Y.

Lyrics from "Mood Indigo," by Duke Ellington, Irving Mills, and Albany Bigard. © 1931 by Gotham Music, Inc. © renewed 1958. Used by permission.

Quotation from "Sexus," Part I of *The Rosy Crucifixion*, by Henry Miller. Obelisk Press, Paris.

"Seesaw Sunday" quotation from "Lament," *The Collected Poems of Dylan Thomas*. New Directions, Inc., New York.

THE last thing she wanted was to start over again with another man. That evening, when the phone rang, she said screw you and ignored it. Not only had her career come to a halt, and her unemployment checks as well, but so had her romance with a night-club comic who suddenly married a singer from Maine after the girl had signed a contract with MGM. Sorrow took hold like heartburn, and she stayed home depressed for weeks. As if this wasn't enough, doom was looming dead ahead in the form of her twenty-eighth birthday.

In the next room, however, the ringing did not stop. Tanya, old girl, you'd better answer it, she thought. With your luck the whole building's on fire, and you without insurance. She trotted in from the kitchen to pick up her phone, the smell of chopped onions on her hand. It was Marcia and Irving Mendelson demanding that she accompany them to a costume ball (they had decided she needed a night out), and she answered with a thanks-all-the-same but that she didn't think she wanted to go. Then Tanya remembered the cig-arette-girl costume she had worn in her scene with Bob Mitchum, and she thought what the hell and said yes.

They arrived in topcoats, though the evening was humid, for it was the only way she and the Mendelsons (who wore Indian out-fits) could get through the streets without causing a commotion. The large second-floor loft, dimmed with blue lights, was uncom-fortably filled with a mumbling crowd. When Tanya removed her coat there was hardly a stir. It was not what she expected; the very opposite, in fact, of all that mad pushing and shoving she had caused at the Artists and Models Ball. She was greatly relieved. Of course her costume this time was less extreme: two stunning shafts of net-stockinged legs and a low bare back. There were many women there in outfits more severe, or at least more bizarre. One of these females, an odd-looking creature in black ankle-length, skintight leotards with matching cape, came forward to welcome them. The only body flesh that could be seen on her were two large diamond-shaped peek-a-boo cuts in the cloth at either side of the pelvic region. "Welcome all," she gushed while exaggerating a curtsy. There was something in the air, something about the whole thing that wasn't right. Tanya was the first to sense it and the first to discover what it was. She checked the other women again carefully. There *were* no other women. There were only men.

When she explained this to the Mendelsons, they found it all very funny, for Irving had got the invitation through a friend of a friend. Marcia thought perhaps they should leave, but Tanya didn't agree. Here was one party in which she was sure to be left alone. Besides, hell, she wanted to watch.

A man with hairy legs, dressed in an angel costume, was explaining that blue was a bad shade for him to a colored Balinese dancer who was listening sympathetically. Marie Antoinette was sitting in a corner waiting for an invitation to dance, his bare arms too bony and his face too manly for the costume. A youth dressed as the devil came over and planted a kiss on the hairy leg of the angel. The man in the black leotard and cape said it would almost be worth taking off his tights for that. Two handsome, almost identical-looking men in blue sweaters and black pants were kissing as they danced. Everywhere, there was indiscriminate laughter.

That was the first thing she noticed about Val: his laugh. To her ears it seemed more genuine, more spontaneous, like that of a playful rascal. At first she thought he was in costume; later she realized that this was just the way he dressed. His black trousers were snug and tapered, with his belt buckled on his left side instead of in front. His shabby suede jacket had its collar turned up as though his back were to the wind, and at his neck swelled a colorful ascot. And that face! So fascinatingly thin and economical that for a while she couldn't look away. Attached to no one in particular, he was now entertaining a small group, relating with wild fervor some fantastic tale that Tanya couldn't quite catch. She had never seen anyone more alive, more enthusiastic, fairly sparkling with some private sort of urgent joy. He actually bounced as he talked, his heels springing up and down with rhythmic excitement. She had never seen anything like it. His hands did a little dance in the air. His face, almost lecherous with rapture, was now wildly grinning, now making an animated point with popping eyes. Yet with all of this there was something double-edged about him, as though he was not only ecstatic, but was making fun of his own ecstasy as well.

"Dig the swinger," Tanya said. "Is he like ever far out?"

Marcia gasped and elbowed her husband. "Irving, will you look who's there."

After they called him over, Val was as ebullient as ever. He had just discovered a book. This was what all the stir was about.

"Not since Dostoyevsky," he cried, "have I been so inundated, so swallowed whole. I tell you this guy's *sublime*. Here's an obscene book written by a saint. No wonder he's on the shit list. And a saint *born* in Brooklyn. Can you imagine? And how wonderfully ironic. The authorities refuse it publication. Wonderful."

Tanya smiled: "I'm by him already curious."

"Yes, who is this great man?" asked Marcia.

"Who *is* he? *Here!*" And he pulled from his pocket a small volume of *Alice in Wonderland*.

"You're kidding," Irving insisted. "In Brooklyn that story takes place?"

Val's answer was to show them the title page. *The Rosy Crucifixion* by Henry Miller. Because Irving was dubious of its quality, Val flashed through the pages until he found the passage he wanted. "Listen to this, you skeptic, you henpecked *Zionist*." He began to read with a stage presence that Tanya was quick to notice.

"'Every day we slaughter our finest impulses. That is why we get a heartache when we read those lines written by the hand of a master and recognize them as our own, as the tender shoots which we stifled because we lacked the faith to believe in our powers, our own criterion of truth and beauty. Every man, when he gets quiet, when he becomes desperately honest with himself, is capable of uttering profound truths. We all derive from the same source. There is no mystery about the origin of things. We are all part of creation, all kings, all poets, all musicians; we have only to open up, only to discover what is really there.'"

Not waiting for their reactions, he continued to skim the pages, reading whatever caught his eye. Tanya was looking at him like a child who had spied a new toy. He didn't take special notice of her, and that *was* intriguing. He was queer all right, but that wasn't the answer. Everyone looked her over, men and women (a condition, both flattering and exasperating, to which she had become addicted), and most of these looks, approving or not, had a definite touch of deference. With Val it was nothing of the sort. He didn't give himself away by appearing overly interested or by posturing no interest at all. His glances at her as well as at the others were alive with curiosity and amusement. It was the amusement that got under her skin.

The next thing she knew they were off on another topic. Marcia had mentioned the costume ball, and Val erupted all over again.

"Isn't this the *wildest*? Look at the joker in green. And how about him there? *God!*" He paused to make way for his own laughter. "Is this your first time at a thing like this? It *is*? Well, you must be having a goddamn *ball*. I know I am. It's good and grotesque and wonderfully evil."

"Crazy," replied Tanya, though it was an effort to remain blasé.

Val wiggled a paper cup. "Empty! Yours, too? Let's fill 'em. Come on."

Almost at once it was an hour later. Val was still going strong. He talked incessantly, laughed uproariously, drank continually, and danced a wild cha-cha with a hand on Tanya's waist. The party had been successfully sidetracked outside the movement of time, and Val was saying: "What a disillusioning age we live in. Christ once turned water to wine, and now it's done each morning by every third-rate French restaurant." While Tanya laughed, she saw the odd-looking creature in the black leotard with matching cape come up and place a hand with its several rings on the shoulder of Val's shabby suede jacket.

"I do hope," the creature gushed, "this divine vision hasn't so beguiled you that you've forgotten all about work, if you'll pardon that nasty word."

"Hell," said Val, "it's a good thing you reminded me." He moved away without further word, sidestepping several couples to get to the door.

"And don't forget to take her," the creature called after him. "She's such" (he turned back to Tanya, his voice modulating) "a truly *divine* vision." And the creature in leotards and the cigarette girl in net stockings nodded graciously at each other, their smiles like uncodable messages exchanged between two distant planets.

Tanya was released from further conversation when Val returned like a quick-change artist, impeded now by a network of wires and straps. His stiff left arm held high the black half-sphere of a strobe light like a burnt-out torch from which a wire dangled down to a battery box that hung by a thick strap from his left shoulder. Another wire from this box made a sagging spiral bridge to his Rolleiflex suspended at his stomach by an ink-stained strap from around his neck.

Val spoke into the ground glass of his camera, the devil smiled, and half of the room was bathed in a curt flash of vanished light. The Balinese dancer was next, then Marie Antoinette, until one by one the most unusual, or imaginative or just outlandish costumes were recorded on film to the general approval of all. He saved Tanya for last, her beauty effortlessly triumphant as she posed in the center of a group picture, the devil and the angel at her feet and the two handsome men in blue sweaters like handmaidens at her side.

By the time the job of photographing the ball was completed, it was late, and the Mendelsons decided it was time to leave; Tanya, with an early rehearsal next morning, agreed. Val surprised her by offering to ride with them uptown. He asked the creature in the black leotard to safeguard his heavy camera equipment, and then he was ready to go.

In the hallway, men standing in twos were talking intimately. One couple was exchanging telephone numbers on the insides of match covers. Some curious girls who had gone up to the loft to watch, were now leaving in annoyance and disgust. A meager, shrivel-lipped redhead called back over her shoulder as they headed down the stairs, "Have a sweet little time. Be good to each other."

It had begun to rain. Val and Irving Mendelson opened their umbrellas, and Tanya thought it was hysterical the way Val held it so high, comically exaggerating its mushroom formality. As he walked and chatted, he pointed out things of interest that caught his attention. Just to be with him was to rediscover in the everyday dull things of a hectic city a charm and significance she had forgotten were there. Occasionally laughing and frequently just listening, she was amazed at him and delighted.

In the IRT it was even better. Val sat with his umbrella hanging from a handstrap while everyone, including strangers, listened as he told of a Harlem party he once attended where he played the bongo drums for a girl from the Broadway show *House of Flowers* who did a barefoot dance to his rhythm. "The outlandishly silly part of it," he laughed, "is that I had never before even *touched* the bongos. Yet there I was, looped, sitting among the very people whose ancestors probably invented the damned instrument. They should have lynched me. But all they did was keep buying me free drinks. Can you imagine? I drank so much I don't remember the whole last part of the evening. They even had to take me home. What fine people!"

Val and Tanya got off together at Forty-second Street, and the Mendelsons waved good-by from inside the moving car, and rode on up to the Bronx. Intrigued by the situation, and drawn, as always, toward the entanglement that was all wrong for her, Tanya had now discovered the perfectly futile, the most ideally impossible romantic dead end of her life. This was what she wanted, this was what she needed at the moment more than anything else, a relationship with the safety valve of sexlessness built in. When he said he would walk her home, she nodded and took his arm. She was happy.

"All these poor people walking in the rain," Tanya said of the crowd as they proceeded up bright Broadway. "Someone should be philanthropic and share his umbrella with them, don't you think?"

Quick to catch her playfulness, he took off in a rush, leaving her stranded in the rain.

The scene that followed was this: an odd-looking youth hurried into the oncoming crowd, his umbrella held for a moment over this man, now that woman, and then this couple, and so on, as he tried to protect everybody in the street. He shared equally, so that no one got more than a second or two of shelter before he hurried on, actually not stopping at all, as he scampered gracefully now to the curb, now close to the building, making his way beneath the cliffs of flickering lights, dumb-founding, frightening, and amusing people as he went.

Tanya caught up with him at Forty-seventh Street just as he was calling out to a pert, passing blonde: "Oh, you *would* have your own umbrella, wouldn't you?"

"Look, buddy," said Tanya out of the side of her mouth, making fists and wagging her extended thumbs, "cut this philanthropic bit. Like *I'm* getting wet."

Val leaned closer, his eyes wide open in false amazement, his head shaking with emphasis and pleasure. "You're not public-*spirited*, that's the trouble. No communal *responsibility*."

"Vot you imply? Vot? I got vit great public spirit. Nyet on you."

They fell into mock argument beneath the marquee of a movie theater while people gathered to watch the sexy girl in the trench coat and the joker who had just cavorted up Broadway.

"Don't be exuberant," Val said, doing the old soft shoe. "You're attracting a crowd."

"Balls. Since I met you I haven't been looked at once." And she fell into step beside him.

They sang "Swanee River" with each trying to upstage the other. Then as Tanya held the umbrella like a parasol and began the lyrics of "In your Easter bonnet with all the frills upon it," and while Val passed the hat (Tanya's beret) and even collected a few coins, a grim police officer pushed his broad blue suit through the crowd and told them to break it up.

In the hallway of her apartment, his thin body bounced enthusiastically on his heels, his not quite adolescent face wise and playful with all those signs of experience etched and carved into it, while tapering fingers busied themselves conducting another story. It involved a Greek sea captain he had once met at three A.M. in a Bowery bar who claimed to have put down a mid-Pacific mutiny by threatening to blow up the ship's cargo of explosives with a cigarette lighter given him by the shipping company as a reward for having the best safety record in the fleet.

When finally he left (without trying to touch her), she hurried to the phone and called the Mendelsons, who had just got in.

"Who *was* that?" Tanya demanded. "And *what* was it?"

"Do you fancy him?" Irving asked.

"Like I fancy him."

"She fancies him. Oi vay."

"Come on, spill it."

"If you think I know anything about this guy, you're crazy."

But after Tanya dug it out of him, it developed that Irving knew a good deal about Val De Franco. The Mendelsons had met him in, of all places, the middle of the Nevada desert. A serious crime wave was taking place in the state that summer and the Mendelsons, on the first cross-country trip, were passing through when they heard first about the epidemic of highway holdups. Each day, front-page stories reported another incident. An auto would be stranded with motor trouble at the side of the deserted highway. A passing motorist would pull up to offer help, only to find too late that the other driver was holding a gun. The police sent out special warnings to the public not to stop on the open highway, and not to help anyone who did. Notices were posted along the roads, and announcements were broadcast on the radio. The Mendelsons, cautious people to begin with, needed no further warning. They stopped on the highway only once in all of Nevada and that was just for a moment to change places at the wheel. When Irving settled into the driver's seat, however, he discovered that the car had stalled; worse, it wouldn't start again. Never before had they heard such a silence as in the middle of that desert. They needed help, but help out there on those roads, in that summer, was not to be had. The only noise was the occasional, almost explosion-like sound of another car passing at seventy miles an hour. Of the sixteen that sped by, not one slowed down. Occasionally, in the instant of passing, they would glimpse a cautious face peering at them as though they were contaminated people. It looked hopeless.

When they were getting desperate enough to consider taking off on foot, a wreck of a '39 Ford with a dangling New York license plate and circular cracks on a smashed windshield came blustering up the road heading east. Before Irving had a chance to wave, the Ford came to a noisy halt behind them. The door beside the wheel wouldn't open, and so the man (now it looked more like a boy) had to climb out the passenger side. He was such a shabby sight with dungarees, T-shirt and unshaven face, that out there in the desert he looked dangerously disreputable. Yet he was so elated, so full of good cheer that Marcia took to him immediately. In ten minutes the stalled engine was roaring again, and the stranger, who said his name was Val, wiped his hands on his dungarees and prepared to depart. Hadn't he heard, asked Marcia, about the holdups? Indeed, he had, in fact, just the other day he was held up himself. A fat man in overalls, standing beside a green station wagon with an open hood, had flagged him down not far from Reno, then pulled a gun. It must have been awful, Marcia said. But to Val it was "a marvelous experience." Never before in his entire life had anything like that happened. Irving wanted to know how much money the man robbed from him. Val's shoulders shook with that silent laughter of his indicating a kind of derisive infatuation with life itself. He hadn't been robbed at all. He had simply talked the gunman out of it. It was the soft sell, Val explained. He and the fat man "chatted" for about twenty minutes. The fat man stood there eyeing a roadside cactus and rubbing his nose with the barrel of his gun. Then, to Val's surprise, he said, "All right, go ahead, get out of here."

"All this," said Marcia, "and you still stopped for us?"

"What the hell. I figured I'd become a roadside evangelist."

"There's money in it," said Mendelson. "Already once you saved all your money."

Again it was good-by, with Val climbing back into his '39 Ford (passenger side first) and they waited to see him off. The car refused to start. Now it was the Mendelsons who offered aid, but the old auto was beyond their help. As he leaned over the fender, toes off the ground, examining the mystery of the engine, Val explained in grunts that he had bought the Ford for only twenty dollars. It had broken down on him just twice while crossing the country. On the way back, though, it was practically coming apart as it moved. Since the end was surely near, he gave a poignant pat to the hood, removed from the back seat a knapsack doctored with adhesive tape, a partly consumed bottle of tequila, a pummeled copy of the poems of Dylan Thomas, and rolled the four-wheeled wreck into the ditch. Then he hitched a ride with the Mendelsons as far as Salt Lake City because he had been reading about Mormonism and the subject so fascinated him that he wanted to see the place.

Aside from the impression he always gave of being perpetually energetic, someone to whom all things and thoughts were of great interest, the Mendelsons felt that there was something elusive about him, something they failed to understand. For example, when it was his turn at the wheel he sped across the Nevada-Utah plains with an odd sort of excitement. It had nothing to do with the juvenile compulsion to race. He drove as though there was some hidden humor in speed, hidden, in fact, in everything, and that only he understood the joke.

First came the surprise of the Salt Flats, looking like a valley of snow in the summer heat. Next, the Great Lake, gray and still; and finally, the amazing cleanliness of the city itself. They stopped right in front of Temple Square, and Marcia leaned forward and Val climbed out. Before they parted, he mentioned he would need a job when he got back to New York, and Irving said he could help out, that he had connections with a bookshop on Fifth Avenue. Though they were certain they would never hear from him again, sure enough, three months later, he phoned.

Val turned out to be one of the best salesmen in the shop. Certain customers soon refused to let anyone else wait on them, and he was just sensational with old ladies who bought almost every book he recommended. It seemed that people were happy just talking with him, and there were customers who came back again and again who had never bought a book until the day they first wandered in and Val came up to them and began to talk. Finally, the manager begrudgingly admitted that Val deserved a raise. Yet on the morning he intended delivering the good news, Val failed to appear. No message of explanation. Nothing. The next day he didn't come to work either. A letter arrived instead informing the management that he had quit. In it Val admitted that he had had a delightful time working at the shop and several most rewarding experiences; nevertheless further association with them would gain him nothing more than a salary, and since he now had enough coin of the realm to last for a while, he was therefore resigning: Thank you and good-by. Even if Val was the best salesman on the floor, the management was still glad to see him go. If there was one thing the boss hated it was a salesman who talked too much, especially if he was a queer.

"But is it true?" Tanya insisted on the phone. "Is he really swish? Yes or no?" She had no idea which answer she preferred.

"Tonight what do you think that place was we were at? A boy-scout meeting for friendly boys?"

"I guess you're right."

"You're asking me? I should be asking you!"

"You mean like did he come on? Uh-uh. No."

"Well?"

"Well?"

"I don't know the answer."

"Neither do I."

Val saw quite a lot of her after that, but he still didn't come on. Not once did he put his arm around her waist, or even hold her hand, though after a while he began giving her an occasional peck on the cheek. Things continued that way until finally, one night, he did kiss her on the lips. It wasn't much different, however, from one of those on the cheek. He didn't do it again.

The romance, such as it was, initiated a change in Tanya's life that was quite startling. Now there were no more periodic skirmishes in the backs of taxis or on the doorstep at an evening's end, no more hand-to-hand struggles to stay in her clothes while visiting the strange apartments of undiscourageable men. Instead, she spent all her time with Val, and this made it seem to her as though a truce had been declared. Mostly, there was just talk: hours and hours of it: and not talk that slithered like a legless thing toward the subject of sex or that was meant to be a stopgap until they were alone, but comfortable talk about photography and acting and God knows what else. The very novelty of it was a pleasure.

This was not to say that life with Val De Franco was lacking in excitement. She found him to be one of the most unpredictable and interesting of men. It was her belief, until they started going together, that she had been taken to every imaginable place of entertainment in and around the City of New York. Night spots, Broadway shows, beach parties, bowling: she had done it all, and she had done it many times. Yet with Val she went down the Hudson from the Cloisters to Bowling Green paddling a kayak which he had borrowed for the day from a half-crazy belt maker on Bleecker Street; with Val she spent hours watching the monotoned tragedies of night court; with Val she visited a monastery in New Jersey where a friend of his was studying to be a Trappist monk; or with Val there was the indulgence of doing nothing, or rather doing just what they wanted, like sprawling out on the Japanese matted floor of her own apartment while she did quick pencil sketches of him snapping black and white shots of her as the rhythms of Gerry Mulligan bounced casually in the background.

Also during the first few weeks Tanya never knew when he was drunk and when he wasn't. He was intoxicated at the most unexpected times. His ability to hold his liquor was astounding, greater than that of anyone she had ever met. In fact, in those earlier days when she was first getting to know him, everything about Val seemed astonishing.

His photographs astonished her, too. Not the picture stories with which he made his living; they dealt with people in unusual occupations, or show business personalities (he did several sets on her alone) or, to make ends meet, "cheesecake." Rarely did she see these, anyway, for he always sent them right off to a photo agency to be developed and sold. The photos she liked best he had done years ago for his own pleasure. He had gone back to doing more of these lately, although there was little market for them. By appearing without pay in some European photo annual they might bring him prestige, but Val had no interest in that. The best of these photographs made a stack of bleed-mounted eight-by-tens in his closet which she discovered and he took out and displayed for her one by one. These were the shots that thrilled her. Bright, bleak, blurred photos of movement in Manhattan. Crowds, traffic, children; the sudden capture of faces unaware; the fast New York scene with a slow blues beat.

She was proud of him. And he was poor, too, which made it almost perfect.

"This is bugging me," she said out loud while alone one evening in her apartment, with her roommate away in Washington for the weekend. She realized it was a game, and that was the trouble. He had made allusions to wanting her but she would banter the idea around until it became harmless. Oh, how she longed sometimes to have a man beside her. Not necessarily beside her for the night, but just to have him handy should the drinks in a dark corner booth of an East Side bar begin to stir in her some extraladylike appetites, just to have within reach a pair of male lips with which to share a moment's indulgence. At such times she would not lean against Val for affection and comfort for she knew he would be unequal to the task of making her loneliness subside, would, in fact, only cause it to increase. Not that Val failed to pay proper attention. He was always quick to appreciate how a dress or a different lipstick did her justice. And if, as sometimes happened, his palm came to rest on her leg as they sat together, she would casually, unreproachfully, tunnel her hand under his. She couldn't take the pretense of his touch for she understood that at such moments he could not feel what his hand was doing.

"This is bugging me," she repeated, and two months to the hour from the day they met, she got up from the Carole Lombard canvas chair, tossed aside the book which had the scene she must memorize for Monday, lit the third cigarette in the last twenty minutes, and told herself it was over.

As soon as one decision was reached another lay just ahead. How was she to break the news to him? Tanya always handled her social problems with a third-act-climax view of life. She detested those "cowardly" women who go about ending an affair by slowly poisoning it to death with indifference or bitchiness and with constant denials that anything is wrong. Anyway. she just loved playing the big scene: though with Val she feared she would be unable to put her heart and talent into it. There was something about this boy that made it difficult for her to be dramatic or even the slightest bit insensitive.

After mixing a drink, she picked up the phone and called him, for now was the time to do it, when her resolve was still warm. When he didn't answer by the third ring she knew he wasn't home. Well, in that case, she would begin by calling up all the men she had stopped seeing and re-enter herself in the social arena. Sitting down, she dumped the phone on her lap and began dialing. But it was Friday night and everyone was out. With irritation and self-pity, she sat sipping her second drink and listening, in far-off, empty apartments, to the sound of barren, merciless ringing. For the past fifteen years, wherever she lived, the phone had never let her alone. Now when she would have welcomed its interrupting ring, when she wanted in the worst way, someone to talk to, it was as though the entire city had been evacuated. Even the Mendelsons were out. She made herself another drink, and in desperation was trying Val's number once again, when all at once there was a friendly rap on her door. She was saved.

He came in wet from a rain she didn't know was falling, carrying a rose he had snatched from a display outside a flower store and, of course, drunk. This last part, she had learned to detect in him from little mannerisms and a slightly intensified gaiety. As she poured him some Scotch, he told her with great animation about a "wonderful little Jap" he had met in Martin's Bar who claimed he had four nipples on his chest and then opened his shirt to prove it.

For Tanya, the first ten minutes took forever. Then all at once it was an hour since he had arrived, and now he was making plans for them to go to Bear Mountain on Sunday. The time had come and she was frustrated. Tell him and get it over with. Yet she cautioned herself not to wound his feelings, for she was really the guilty one, the one who had started it all in the first place by keeping company with a queer.

"Like, I'm not coming to Bear Mountain with you, Val," she said. "Not there, baby, nor anywhere else with you any more."

Too abrupt and she knew it. He looked up from his drink, eliminating this time the habitual brushing back of his hair that now needed cutting so badly.

"I know this sounds sick the way I'm throwing it at you. Val, it's been a ball. I mean it. We really swung. But from the beginning like we knew we couldn't work out, didn't we? I'm sorry. I really am sorry. I'm sorry, Val."

He peered vacantly at her from the floor where he sat. He was propped against the couch in the posture of a ventriloquist's dummy whose owner had just left the room. His face turned to white plaster and his voice to deep sarcasm as he gave his reply.

"Poisoning my drink would be the perfect dra*mat*ic touch. Or perhaps you thought of that?"

"I'm trying to be serious, Val."

"You're right. Poison *is* sort of comic-bizarre nowadays."

"*Val.*"

"I suppose you prepared an appropriate monologue for the occasion. Spill it. I won't upstage you. It should be interesting. I'm all *ears.*"

She estimated he had been bar-hopping for hours; however, after three drinks she felt she had caught up with him. Though his contempt frightened her, now was not the time to stop and besides liquor had put a comic costume on both of them, dramatic climax or not. Across the courtyard a saxophone climbed into a passage of "Frenesi" and then dropped out of it and did a B-flat scale. She hoped that the liquor wouldn't garble her words. She sat up straight and looked at him. She explained that she was in need of a relationship that was complete; one that would build toward something; not one like theirs. In life as in show business, a woman, at twenty-eight, unless she has staked a claim, has a way of running out of time. Since there was no future between them she would have to look for one somewhere else. She knew, in a way, it was her fault. This relationship, she explained, was unethical. She had told herself that it was her welfare with which she was concerned; her future that must be considered. But another reason she couldn't allow this thing to go on was her fear that if they continued together as they were doing, it would be his life, too, that would be wasted.

"Be honest with yourself and you'll understand me," she said, noticing his puzzled look. Then she amazed herself by adding: "Like I'm a chick who digs sex."

"You can dig it in my flower box any time," he replied, flippant again about love in that way of his she always hated.

"Can I? Right now?"

Her legs in knit slacks were tucked under her in the armchair. The alto sax rushed into "Frenesi" again and then stopped completely. In the rain pipe there was the unhurried tapping of water.

"Right now? Hell, sure. Any time."

"I mean *now!*" Her hands, suspended in the air, were those of an orator.

"Exactly what point are you trying to belabor?"

Her patience was taking flight. "Do I have to spell it out? Are you ready to, you know, make it with me today, this evening, or not?"

"A little *lou*der and we'll dance to it."

"I'm waiting for like an answer. An answer."

"Yes, damn it, right now."

His insistence on his own normality was torture for her. At last, with great relief, she lost her temper.

"This is bugging me," she shouted. "Stop the pretense, will you?" Moving now across the room, one of her high heels sounded a single rap on the margin of wooden floor between two scatter rugs. "Do you think I'm a moralist? Do you think I'm going to reproach you?" She spun away to jab her cigarette into a table ashtray and whirled back again. "A person can go this way or that way or both ways. You think I care? You think I give a shit? Let's face our feelings, buddy. Let's stop pretense." She knelt in front of him on the floor holding closed with her right hand the neck of her white blouse. "I'm not putting you down, Val, but we're like not the same, you and me. Are we? Damn it, are we? We can't make the same scene. Admit. it. For crying out loud, admit it."

Sitting Indian-style with elbows on his knees, Val watched his stiffened palms roll back and forth, his drink pressed between them. He did not bother with the hair hanging over one eye as his head shook up and down in sluggish agreement.

With a breath of relief, Tanya collapsed in the armchair and let her head go loose on her neck. "Well, that's it then. Here we are."

The sax player was doing a slow several minutes of a song that was familiar but which she couldn't place.

"Would you mind if we talked about this a little?" she asked, now that everything had been pulled out into the open and was lying there civilized and harmless.

"Crazy. Why not."

As the languorous saxophone went into the refrain, a junction of thought and sound was reached in her mind and suddenly she knew what song it was. The familiar notes had transformed themselves into the words

> *That's why I ask the Lord*
> *in Heaven above,*
> *What is this thing called love?*

She whispered "too much" into her glass and then aloud, repeating what he had said: "Crazy. Why not…. Okay, I've always been curious. If you want to talk about it. Like how far back can you remember being this way?"

His brow wrinkled. "What way?"

"Aw, come on, buddy. No pretense, remember?"

"I don't get you."

"That goddamn ball." (It was an expletive she had picked up from him.) "That's what I mean. Those people there. Those men."

"So?"

"So? So like you're one of them, aren't you?"

"One of them? Hell and Holy Jesus, woman. So that's what this goddamn thing's all about. Listen, for crysake, don't try to make a queer out of me just because you're a dyke."

Tanya flung out an astonished and indignant "*What!*" The word had started as a laugh and ended in an open-mouthed scowl.

"Now don't blow your wig when you're the stupid bitch who brought it up."

"Me? A Lesbian?"

"Well?"

"Man, wherever did you get *that* loony idea?"

"At the costume ball. Somebody pointed you out. That was my impression, too. And it made sense 'cause, baby, you turned out to be the chilliest doll this side of the Arctic Circle."

"*I* was chilly?" she yelled at him, springing to her feet. "*You* were chilly. Like you never even *kissed* me."

"Kiss *you?* I couldn't even *touch* you without chancing frostbite."

"You mean to tell me you're not…a queer?"

"Oh, hell, woman."

"But Irving Mendelson said so."

"That orthodox son-of-a-bitch. What does he know from fancy perversions?"

Cornered by confusion, Tanya's mind hurried back, gathering memories in a frenzy, trying to re-evaluate everything she could remember about him, but it was, of course, too much to do at once and came to nothing.

"I think you're lying," she concluded. "Go on, you're lying."

"Then try me."

"You're ready right now?" She was furious with bewilderment.

"Ready, on your mark."

"Right now?"

"Right now."

"Well, come on," she snapped at him as she stood there. Neither of them moved.

Tanya pulled off her white blouse and threw it away. Her bra was white against her sleek cinnamon skin. She was no longer an actress playing a scene. She was too involved for that, and all at once everything she did or said had a savage sincerity.

"I got to know," she cried. "I'm waiting."

A look of regret, almost unwillingness, fastened itself to his features. Dawdlingly he got to his feet, and she decided he was stalling. He strolled toward her and her verdict was bravado. His face held a perpetual wince and she judged it fear. Nevertheless, she backed away.

"I want you to stop it," she yelled. "Don't play games." Her back came up against the off-white living-room wall. "You're pretending, aren't you? Don't experiment on me, you hear? Will you please stop it."

This man, or whatever he was, made as if to touch her. Never before had she experienced such ambivalence. Her unwillingness came to the surface with a tremble. In the semilight, his face was boyish and sinister and more incomprehensible than ever. It was as though he were striving to hold back a convulsion. While a gargle of thunder rolled over the city, he reached out a second time. She said no by swinging her head back and forth, her eyes rolling in their sockets as they remained fixed upon him. The electric storm coming at the city from the south stirred the room with a cool column of air. In the gentle disturbance, the lone, driftwood lamp appeared somehow to burn less brightly, its protectiveness diminished. He took from the nearby table a pair of scissors which she had used that very afternoon to slice through the uncut pages of a book of plays by Pirandello. The muscles of her back were made rigid with terror. Then, confronted by the presumptuous idea that he might be trying to kill her, she grew surprisingly calm. She watched the scissors getting closer, and waited to see what would happen. They were as incomprehensible as the man who was about to use them. They opened and became two knives, they touched her with a cold blade, and then they closed with a flourish. It was surprising how clean and forcibly they cut right through the middle strand of her white brassiere, causing it to part and fall to the floor like some strange dead bird.

She could see the point where the two walls and ceiling joined. Her head was slightly elevated as she lay in silence on the couch, her right shoeless foot pointing at the bleak pocket formed by the joining walls and ceiling. Aiming her big toe, she slowly traced the line at the top of the front wall. Plaster cracks, like brunette hair strands, marred the ceiling and, in some way, the silence as well. Part of a painting could be seen: rough, brittle, fatigued. She shifted her position in the dry silence, the bitter cold still clinging to her body. Minutes earlier it had grabbed her by the scruff of the neck thrusting its chilling strength under her dress. Now a radiator was making sounds like a sick kitten. It was December first. She felt the terrible absence of human noise.

"I don't know, I really don't." She lifted her head a moment to smooth her hair. "Am I a good actress, a bad actress or what? I feel so worthless, as worthless as I did as a child. In this film I have to scream. In bright sunlight I walk along the white wall in a white slip feeling the stucco surface with my hands. Then I scream. I turn as the camera dollies in, and I keep screaming. Oh, it's a fun scene. But the trouble is I couldn't do it. I yelled all right. That's the trouble, it's a yell, not a scream. I simply couldn't bring it out. The director had me try it again and again. Everyone else was waiting for the next scene. God, I felt so inadequate. Mechanical is the word.

For the next bit I had to put on blackface. It's a crazy, surrealistic film, this *Superego*. In a way it would be fun to make if the director wasn't out to make me as well. Anyway, I put on blackface and this wild blond wig, and I begin scrubbing the floor of this room. Then a blind man comes tapping his way in and sets fire to the bookcase. It's like wild, boy. Too much. So while I'm putting on the blackface I remember the days when I was a child, and my mother tried to bleach my skin because she thought I looked too Italian, and so what do I do? I start to cry. You know, just sitting there crying as I put on my makeup. I tell you I'm coming apart. God, what a bitch she was, my mother. What a stupid, intolerant bitch. I guess we're not all lucky enough to be orphans. Wow, if I had a dollar for all the times she called me a slut I'd be rich. I'd still be neurotic but I'd be rich. And that's the difference between Val and the others. I don't feel any of this business with him. With him I don't feel like somebody's going to tap me on the shoulder and say, 'O.K. Miss, come along with us. We've caught you, you fraud.' "

"With him, though, you feel superior."

The voice broke in on her with a slight shock, and Tanya realized that she had been talking with her eyes closed. The two walls and the ceiling reappeared, so did the painting, so did a window on the left, its blinds partly drawn, beyond which she saw the dim suggestion of brick.

"Yes, I guess so. With him all my feelings seem so sharply edged. I feel hate, too, real hate sometimes, and it frightens me. I wonder like where's all the love I'm supposed to feel for him."

The voice broke in again from behind. "It's appropriate to experience anger toward someone close to you. If you can't feel anger you won't feel love."

"Well, I must really be in love then by the way I want to, you know, like kill. It's heart-warming, I tell you. Six months now we've been seeing each other, and what a mixture of feelings. What a mess. He's so hard to describe. There's a sense of, what is it? Amorality, I guess. A sense of amorality about him. Sometimes I don't think he takes anything seriously. Other times he seems in a vague, constant, undefined rage. It kills me. He's very inconsiderate at times and at other times terribly loving. He used to be an actor, you know. He spends hours and hours with me going over a scene or helping me memorize my lines. He knows that the most important thing in the world for me is to achieve recognition as an actress. So he helps whenever he can. I care so much about my work, but the funny thing is he doesn't care at all about his. He's a great, great photographer who wastes his talents. Really. Many people tell me how fine he was when he was first starting out, and I know 'cause I've seen his work. He doesn't care. Doesn't care at all. Oh, I don't know. He's a schmuck. Sometimes I think I love him just because he's so hard to get to. If that's so, then I'm following the same old pattern. I've tried to talk him into analysis. He just laughs."

"You must let him know your needs. Tell him he's evasive. Keep pointing it out to him when he's destructive to the relationship. You must fight for what you want. You might lose him by doing it. But the way he is now, he's a dangerous guy for you."

"I know, and yet I feel so good with him. Not like I've felt since I can't remember when. Yesterday, for example. I must tell you this so you don't think it's all bad between us. Yesterday, for example, he cooked for me. He's a marvelous cook. It was his thirtieth birthday. Anyway he had me over to his place. That one-room mess of his for twenty-four a month on Elizabeth Street. Yet I like being there somehow. He had bought me a present. A bottle of pills, you know, pregnancy pills from the Margaret Sanger Institute. The idiot. It was all gift-wrapped and everything. And a card saying one a day keeps the doctor away. We had a marvelous feast. Drinks before, wine during, brandy after. Candlelight and music. Really it was marvelous. One candle was burning, both radiators were going, and I felt so happy I wanted to dance. When he took my dress off he said he wasn't seducing me, just stealing my clothes. He held me in his arms until my cold skin felt warm, then he undid my bra and tossed it on top of a floor lamp. Looking at my breasts he began quoting Shakespeare: 'Whose high upreared and abutting fronts the perilous narrow ocean parts asunder.' And when he said 'parts asunder' he poured the last little bit of his wine down my front and tried to drink it. We showered together, and then we got into his great big bed. He says it's an authentic brass bed from a New Orleans bordello. Oh, it's great to be completely free with someone, and I felt such love for him. He began at my feet using his tongue between my toes, and when he made love to me he did it as he always does, as though he's never done it before with me or with anyone else for months. He's so good. He's a great one on positions. Then, afterward, he puts on the lamps and sets up the camera. He wants to take pictures of us. He sets the self-timer, then runs and jumps in beside me. He wants pictures of us pretending to make love but I wouldn't let him. He's like nuts sometimes, really. In the morning I woke up late and he's already gone to work. There's a note hanging from the electric light cord. It's all about how marvelous he thinks I am in bed. A kind of prose poem signed V. D. Ha, sometimes he's just too much. Then there's a knock on the door that scares the life out of me. Who is it? A good-looking redhead. *'Oh,'* she says, real surprised. Me, I'm half undressed. Then she asks me if Mr. Valentine De Franco is in. Who shall I say called? 'Francheska,' she says. 'Francheska Luca.' How do you like that? I don't know whether to belt her or wait till he comes back and belt him. You know, like who the hell *is* this girl? Is she grabbing some on the side or what? It's so like him. Then I feel hate. I feel like wrecking the place, but it's such a mess anyway he'd never know the difference. God, he infuriates me sometimes. I ask myself why do I take it? Why do I keep seeing him? I know he won't marry me. He's already half said as much. Doesn't believe in marriage. One of *those* types. It's sick. And yet—and this is what kills me—and yet he's so goddamn sweet. Once we took the Mendelsons' little girl to the museum. We were like mother and father, he and I. He was so good with the child. Patience? I was amazed. Yet, crazy as ever. He was holding Jessica in his arms, and he came up to this fourteenth-century painting of Christ on the cross. The child says, 'Uncle Val, who is that?' And Uncle Val very, very seriously says: 'He was a teacher.' 'What happened to him?' says Jessica. And very solemnly Val says: 'He didn't publish.' I'm laughing, but I should be crying. I love him. I hate him. I don't know. I just don't know."

Santa Claus stood in tired fraudulence in front of Stern's department store ringing a bell with a listless lift and fall of his arm, his eyes staring across the street at the gloom settling in the public park. A woman choir through a crackling loudspeaker sang, "Deck the halls with boughs of holly, Fa la la la la, la la la la," as Tanya, hugging her coat about her, headed east, grinning at the apathetic Santa pillow-packed like a pregnant woman. She remembered a time once when he flew over roof-tops with miraculous reindeer, depositing presents for all. Now he stood begging pennies on Forty-second Street.

But her happiness today was imperishable. It even made her courageous and she jaywalked fearlessly through the tangle of traffic, drawing whistles from a crowded car of Dartmouth students and a reprimand from a Checker-cab driver. She emerged on the other side smiling without knowing it and feeling her coat pocket to see if the long thin package was still there.

From inside the magazine-shingled newsstand, a face with skullcap and earmuffs said, "What's yours, Miss?" and disappeared as soon as she told him, while Tanya waited studying a puckering Tanya in bold Ektachrome on the face of *Escapade* magazine wearing a partly opened negligee that Val had posed her in some months ago. The face with earmuffs reappeared with a folded copy of *Variety*, and the shoulders gave only a slight shrug when Tanya tapped the picture of herself with a red fingernail and said: "You know, I just don't understand how a woman can pose like that?"

In the taxi she gave the address on Elizabeth Street and restrained herself from asking the driver to hurry. From her coat pocket she removed and opened the little box and took out and handled the watch with delicate care. Its handsome leather strap and its heaviness spoke to her of the tactile richness of the male. She kissed it, and sat deliciously happy with the intimacy of her gift. Its beauty and expense would surely bring him closer. "You're wonderful," he'd say to her. "You're generous and thoughtful and loving and..."

"Whoja think y'are, the Voigin Mary?" shouted the driver, and she looked up startled to see, promenading across their path, a fat woman who seemed unmindful of the on-coming cars. "She must think she's immortal," he added, racing forward then braking hard at the next light.

Tomorrow would be an off-white Christmas, for the snow had fallen a few days too early. Yet this made no difference to Tanya, who each year cherished the season anew with a reformed Jew's bipartisan delight. To her it was a free-for-all of infatuation, and she was counting on this evening, Christmas Eve, to inflate Val's heart and set afloat in him a permanent need for her permanent love. She was happily in cahoots with Santa, Christ, and an Elgin watch.

"You a model or actress uh somethin'?"

"Heavens to Betsy. I'm married and a mother of four children."

She tried to look at him; the back of his head was in front of her, his photo on the glove compartment, his eyes in the rearview mirror.

"It's a good ting. I had dis model last week, you know? The call was for some swank place in the east Eighties. I tell ya she cried all der way, all der way. Smashed up over somethin' and such a beautiful girl, too."

"It happens," said Tanya, bemused at her own profundity.

"Be lucky for whatchyare," he said, turning the wheel. "That's what I say. Be lucky for whatchyare."

The building affronted her with its usual smells of dust and dried urine and with its dankness and poverty. Yet she couldn't wait to enter. She hated the indignity of its thin walls, its prison portals of chopped-liver brown, its ancient twirl-lever doorbells. Yet she longed to climb its stairs. The first floor gave off sounds of a family feud. The second landing had no lights. The third, a broken bag of garbage. She ran up the fourth flight to the first door on the left and knocked, smiling, checking the gift in her coat pocket. She touched her hair. She waited, shuffled, listened, knocked, worried, checked the time (six forty-five), and knocked harder. The plan was to meet at his pad at six thirty, dine in Chinatown at eight and attend a party in Brooklyn Heights at ten. "Let us meet at some mutually agreed-upon place," he had said, "like my bed." Also he had said: "We'll have drinks and eat and party-go and if worse comes to worst, we'll make out." Could he be sleeping? She knocked hard and long. The door opened behind her to reveal a kitchen tub, the sound of Stan Lomax with the sport news and a man in suspenders who frowned and retreated. Damn you, Val De Franco, for being late. She rested her chin on the paper column formed by the rolled copy of *Variety*, leaned against the wall and waited. Half an hour later she marched into a phone booth at the rear of the local social club and called her answering service who had received no messages, her agent who had received no messages and the Ulysses S. Hill photo studio. At last! Yes, Val had called. He was tied up on a job and wanted her to meet him at the studio instead. She explained, with a touch of anguish, that she was all the way down at his place, but there was nothing much Ulysses could do. There wasn't even a way she could reach Val.

"Oh, screw it. All right I'll schlepp up there. Tell him to wait."

"You mean he hasn't come yet?" she cried, as she marched in high heels into the empty studio anteroom with its slanting linoleum floor. "This is the third time he's done this to me in a month. And you, what in hell are you doing open on Christmas Eve?"

"Business, believe it or not," said Ulysses Hill from behind his desk wearing, as he always did, a short-sleeved, paisley sport shirt. He was a cautious, gray-haired overworked Negro of fifty-eight years with whom Tanya did business and loved dearly.

"You've got guys coming here to shoot broads on Christmas Eve?" She was amazed. "What are the girls wearing? Net stockings and a Santa hat? Oh, my God, you're kidding? You mean I guessed it right? Wow-wee-wee-wee-wow. Too much."

The neon light outside sent into the room an intermittent flow of garish red. For half an hour the two of them sat and talked until Val bounced in, late and carefree. His excuse was elaborate, his

26

enthusiasm contagious, and soon Tanya was seduced into a kiss. Val shouldered his strobe and camera again, and they left as the first of the customers mounted the stairs. A businessman in rimless glasses was the first to emerge from the street, short of breath but jovial. Recognizing Tanya, he asked if she was posing that evening. She said no and, when he asked why, she said it was because of the occasion. What occasion? Hanukkah, she said.

It was not particularly cold, and in Times Square all that was left of the snow was small mounds of grayish soot at the bottoms of trash baskets and streams of muck along the curb. Festive carols were piped into the street from the doorways of record stores, and each window display wished all and sundry, friend and stranger, thief and saint, Jew and gentile, distributor, consumer, and competitor alike an ornamented, cotton-lettered MERRY CHRISTMAS—HAPPY NEW YEAR.

At Broadway, Tanya took hold of Val's arm and asked him what Ulysses meant by a parting remark tossed after them down the stairs. "Hope you're giving it plenty of thought," the Negro had yelled, his voice amplified in the hall so that it took on a tone of pontifical doom.

"Give what some thought?" she asked, feeling her coat for the present.

"He's a crazy man, is what he is. Wants me to take over the studio. To buy it from him. He wants to retire and be with his daughter."

"I didn't know that. But this is a great opportunity for you, no? It could free you from all this cheap hackwork. You could concentrate on more serious things."

"Are you two in cahoots? He said the same damn thing."

"Could you afford to like buy him out?"

"Are you kidding?"

"Could you raise the money?"

"I suppose so."

"Well, why don't you? Really? It's a wonderful chance. Oh, I get excited just thinking about it. If you don't take it you're like mishiga in the head."

"You love it so much, why don't *you* buy him out?"

"Val, come on. Why not?"

"I'll tell you. But then we shut up about it, all right?"

"All right."

"I don't want his place sitting on my back. I don't want to worry about it or be tied down to it. I want to come and go as I please. O.K.? O.K."

Tanya hit him on the arm with her rolled-up *Variety*. "Fear of responsibility," she cried, "lack of drive. It's the same old story."

He steered her into a doorway and up to a crowded bar. "Jack Daniels straight, please, and hemlock for the lady."

Muffled and frustrated by their abortive conversation, Tanya decided that now was the time to bestow her gift, to preempt his flightiness with her resolve. Then she would cleverly reopen the discussion. Hell, if she was going to marry the man, she wanted him at least to have a steady job. But before giving him her love all wound up in an Elgin watch, she decided first to make the bastard jealous. He was too damn sure of himself as it was.

Lo and behold, standing to her left was this thin-lapelled youth who proved quite willing to be crowded into conversation. She openly admired his nondescript tie and laughed at his quick jokes while to the right of her, busily absorbed in the pages of *Variety*, stood a disinterested Val. They were on their third round of drinks when Val finally leaned over and whispered into her ear. Did she prefer he disappear and leave her alone with Thin Lapels?

Tanya bit into a brittle pretzel. "Hy don't know vot you mean. Hy'm only beink buddy-buddy vit za masses."

Ten minutes later it seemed to grow warmer at the bar, and she removed her coat (Thin Lapels helping, of course) and revealed her apricot knitted dress with its high, upreared and abutting fronts.

"Why don't you and I go bar-hopping together?" asked Thin Lapels to which Tanya replied in all innocence: "Like I don't think my escort would care for that."

"You don't have to worry about him. He left already."

Her eyes checked the bar mirror and there beyond the bottled rows of booze, between the cotton-lettered SEASON'S GREETINGS, was the space where Val no longer stood. Her eyes cut a path through the faces and the smoke and found nothing Val-like anywhere. Clutching her coat, she dashed into the darkness to plunge a look down and then up the cold street. It was hopeless: too much crowd, too much confusion. Which way to run? Looking back into the window of the bar as though hoping someone would give her a hint, she saw his narrow, felonious face. It was poised as if to grin, yet puzzled, hair askew, in his hand a hot dog.

Walking back in, she never felt more like an utter ass in her whole life. At the food counter, she buried her face in Val's shoulder, and he offered his frankfurter and kissed her hair. She clung to his thin rib carriage and peeked at herself in the wall mirror. She was no less lovely. She took courage. Then, checking fearfully, she felt for the gift in her pocket.

"I bad girl," she said. "Tried to get thin, hero-type jealous."

"I know," he mumbled, his mouth occupied with meat, roll, and mustard.

She finished the other half of his frank in the cab. Was now the time, she wondered, to inflict her gift on him? No, she decided to wait for the intimacy of his apartment. With the meter ticking, with his watch in her pocket ticking, with the sweet whiskey sours in her life's blood ticking, she took time out to adore his nicely emaciated, oddly attractive, inward-thinking face. Why doesn't he kiss me? The cab rounded another corner and pressed them together. Now's his chance. Why doesn't he kiss me? the crummy bastard. At last she got through to him, but somehow he received the wrong telepathic message and became suddenly undergraduate and physical. He closed two fingers pincerlike on her leg and she jumped mightily. He palmed her breast, pulled her close, squeezed and grabbed while she roared in a desperate whisper for him to stop. Then he leaned back and sang bawdy songs loudly.

For Tanya, it was a long ride. In the familiar hallway of dust and dried urine, the whiskey sours got her playing with the idea of making love before making dinner. But Val had become teasingly diabolical. On the third landing, he started tightrope walking the banister while the bottomless doom of the silent stairwell waited. Tanya backed into the wall with horror. She covered her eyes and begged him to stop. Yet, with strobe and camera dangling, he persisted until he had climbed to the floor above. Unable to watch and sick with fear, she turned away and waited until she heard his door unlock.

"You know I can't stand you doing that," she cried, entering after him with her pain and fury. The phone interrupted, and before she knew it, he was involved in a carefree discussion with someone called Tiger. Still in her coat, she dropped disgruntledly onto his broken sofa, hugging herself in a posture of homicidal repose. His room was a mess, as usual, and overheated as well. Dramatically she threw open a window (the chained weights knocking) and, removing her coat, went back to playing solitaire with her anger. And just last week he had been so tender. Up yours, she thought, glaring at him. He wasn't looking. He was standing without shoes on the bed, removing his tie and telling the phone any number of charming things.

When he finally saw Tanya's face, Val told Tiger that he would call her back. He bounced down into a sitting position and grinned at her angry silence. She lit a cigarette. Did she have one for him? No, she didn't. The pack was empty and she crushed it with great satisfaction. Before she knew it, he had rustled up something to smoke from the troublesome bottom drawer of a vibrating bureau. Putting on a new shirt, he chatted away about this and that, skating effortlessly across the surface of her hardened mood. When he inhaled, he sucked loudly on his cigarette as though each drag might be the last of his life, holding in the smoke as long as he could and puffing out nothing noticeable.

"Why did you do that on the banister? You know what it does to me."

"Teasing," he explained, scratching his ankle.

"You know I'm terrified of high places."

"Teasing." He shrugged. "Just teasing."

"Don't do it, ever. Promise me, Val? Please?"

"All right, I won't do it ever."

"You're not taking it seriously."

"I am taking it seriously."

"You promise?"

"I promise."

"Like, thanks," she said, bitingly.

"You're quite welcome, I'm sure."

He squeaked on his cigarette, lungs expanding.

"You're very high, aren't you?"

"Sure am," he said.

"On those few drinks?"

"Of course not. Say, your legs look good, you know." He patted a space next to him on the bed.

"You were drinking *before* we met?" she said, not moving from the couch. "I thought you were on a job?"

"I *was* on a job, you silly broad. But afterward I took my client out for a drink."

"Your *client?*" She mocked the neuter gender of the word, as though trapping him in a lie.

"You want more details? All right, she's a Negro Lesbian with masochistic tendencies who once stripped at Minsky's, finishing her number while standing on her head singing 'Three Coins in the Fountain.' She's got a great act, and I took her out afterward for a drink because she cooperated so well … with the posing."

"And meanwhile I was sitting on my ass waiting for you for three-quarters of an hour. What I'd like to know is why the hell are you so inconsiderate? Why? Really, Val, don't you give a damn for me? Forget me. Don't you give a damn for anyone?"

"What's eating you today? I got held up. It happens."

"So put yourself out. For once in your life put yourself out and come on time. With you it's like nothing but tzurus, morning, noon, and night."

His neck tightened, his jaw protruded as he drew on his cigarette with strained effort. He held the smoke in, mouth open, eyes closed. The exhale was a ghostly vapor.

"You are inconsiderate, Val. You are."

Looking at the ceiling, shrugging, palms out, he gave the appearance of great contentment.

"Val, we never talk seriously."

"Why should we? You only get unhappy."

"Oh, shut up."

"She tells me to shut up."

Christmas Eve inched its way forward in the silence. Leaning his chin on his lifted knee, he looked solemn and remote. Sometimes the bones of his face seemed to her to be the form and substance of an early pain that had since cooled and hardened.

"Do you think I'm beautiful?" she asked.

"The only thing that exceeds your beauty is my appreciation of it."

"Do you love me?"

"I do love you."

"You're like full of shit."

They sat facing each other and out of reach. The evening wasn't ruined, wasn't broken beyond repair. It had just suffered a few fractures which she felt she could make well once again.

"I have something for you," she said, reaching for her coat.

He didn't seem to hear.

"Sweetheart."

"Yes?"

"I have something for you."

"For me? Ah, you're a bountiful wench both in body and soul."

His lips tightened on the cigarette again, the tip flaring, the faint, cutting smell of it rising through her nostrils to the roof of her head. Her arm was lifted toward the ceiling holding the coat by the collar as she searched for the correct pocket. She paused.

"Is that…? Val, are you smoking pot?"

"It's Christmas," he assured her.

"Val…" Her frustration almost blocked out her anger. "Val, I'm furious. I am furious."

"Oh, I'm sorry. You want a drag?"

"You know goddamn well I don't want a drag." She was on her feet. "You can choke on it, for all I care." Spiked heels strode the narrow room and back. Firm hands on apricot hips. A voice strong with fervor. "This is *so* like you. One insult after another. One after another. I can hardly keep score. You *know* what this does to you. We have dinner to eat and a party to go to. And you? Where will you be? You'll be drifting around in your little wind-blown world." She sat down. "Why are you doing this? You swore to me."

His brow was furrowed. "Like I said. It's Christmas."

She sat on the edge of the couch as though to pounce. "You care about nothing. Ab-solute-ly *nothing*. I've never met anyone like you. You can't enjoy a thing unless it's evil or scandalous or sacrilegious or illegal. You're like immoral, is what you are. Your drinking, your smoking, your dirty books. And your friends! God, like now there's a motley crew. Junkies, prostitutes, jailbirds, the whole bit. And you, you hide. I see it now. You run away from everything. The great uncommitted man, that's you. Like where do you stand, buddy? Disarmament? Fallout? Where are you? You don't live on this earth, do you? Like what do you care? Let the world blow itself to pieces. Concerned, you're not. You can always sit in the corner with a bottle of booze or a bag of pot or some Negro stripper with masochistic tendencies, and the world can go screw. And married? Like you'll never get married. It's too square. Middleclassville. The only reason you'd get married is so you could commit adultery. And children? Having children is normal, so of course you don't want any. That is unless you could turn your little ones into junkies and prostitutes. Then it might appeal to you. God, you're like so wrong for me I don't even know why the hell I even waste words on you."

Resting his elbows on his knees, staring at the floor, he ground his ashes into the scatter rug with a shifting heel. He spoke without looking up as though he were a decade away.

"Aye, it's a bawdy planet."

Then he stretched out on the bed and studied her.

"You know something, Tan? You want to know something? You have a fine figure, that you do." Fingers plowed through his

33

hair. "I love your skin texture, do you know that? They should try to make wallpaper like it. Wouldn't that be a gas? Skin-textured wallpaper."

"Val, where arc you?"

"It would be a gas, all right."

"Val, were you listening to me?"

"Then it would make some sense."

"What would make sense?"

"The expression."

"What expression?"

"Climbing the wall."

"Val…"

"For example: I was climbing the wall last night. It's skin-textured, you know."

She went and sat next to him.

"Val, where the hell are you? I don't know where you are!"

He pointed, dropping ashes in his hair. "I'm up there in the corner by the ceiling."

She had lost him, and it had all happened so quickly.

"It's skin-textured, you know." He laughed and the hilarity began to grip him. "It's skin-textured, you know."

"Please, Val. Stop it."

"It's skin-textured, you know. Ha, ha. It's skin-textured, you know." And on he went like a damaged record reiterating a foolish selection of sounds. He would hold up his finger, lift up his head, speak his line, laugh and fall back overcome by its startling novelty. He continued this precisely the same way twenty times over.

"Val, you're hung up. Stop it. *Val.*" Then screaming: "VAL!"

"It's skin-textured, you know."

She was on her feet and using her fist, moving awkwardly, she struck at his leg. Tears had taken possession of her face; streaks of pain reflecting the bulb in the ceiling. "Don't do this to me," she yelled in misery. After several more screams, she stopped exhausted and wretched, listening to his doomed repetitive laughter, to his now fully meaningless joke made torturous and vapid by eternal rediscovery. As she cried softly to herself, a cold tear fell half her height into her hot palm.

Released from himself, he lay for a while on the bed watching (though his lids were closed) the circular light fixture on the ceiling above him. One bulb lit, one dead, one missing. He jackknifed into a sitting position. *Missing.* His eyes made a rapid check of the room, cutting a path through the fog. *Variety* lay curled on the table. He dashed into the bathroom and then out and into the hallway, plunging a look down the vast stairwell. It was hopelessly silent and empty. He called loudly. Upon the dim landings and into the dark corners of the building below, his voice fell and died.

She had come all the way uptown in the bitter cold, entered the elevator, was carried to the eleventh floor, followed the noise to one of the doors, and there lost courage. She listened to the muffled gibberish of a party in full swing—a square uptown party at that—and regretted having left her apartment on this the worst night of the year. The passageway was like a tomb with sounds of life heard somewhere beyond. She decided not to join the living, to flee instead, but by then it was too late. The elevator had been called down to the main floor and was climbing again, perhaps with a carload of guests, to this very floor. Her fear grew as the car came to a stop, emitting party noises of its own. The door opened amid crashing laughter. To escape, Tanya pushed into the apartment and became one of fifty people, each with a drink and something to say. Floating above it all in a sophisticated mood of ennui was the all-pervasive voice of Frank Sinatra.

> *When you said good-by, love,*
> *What had we to gain?*
> *When I gave you my love*
> *Was it all in vain?*

Irving Mendelson touched her cheek with a disturbingly asexual kiss. Marcia ran out of the blur and embraced what her husband had just relinquished. Her lips were harmlessly loving, and Tanya hugged her back. Coat removed, the newcomer stood modestly in a black dress and black shoes looking sad and sensational and a bit lost.

"I was afraid you weren't coming," said Marcia, "and after all our persuasion."

"You're looking very good," said Irving, supportively.

"Yes, you are," Marcia agreed, protectively.

"You really are," they both added with solicitous grins.

"I don't know how long I'll stay," Tanya explained. "I…"

"Oh, come on now," Irving interrupted, taking her arm, giving her some Scotch in a paper cup, and steering her toward the main room.

"He's here," said Marcia, taking her other arm.

Tanya's whole body twinged. "Who? Who's here?"

"Dexter Morganstern. We told you about him. He always wanted to meet you but you were … you know …"

"Tied up," Irving suggested to get all three of them through the sentence.

"Don't introduce me," Tanya pleaded. "If things happen, then let them happen. I mean, like where's the john?"

Making her way down the hall, Tanya saw a high blonde turn to someone and say: "Botticelli is a cheese, you idiot, not a wine."

The bathroom mirror told its usual flattering lie, and Tanya, not taken in, wasted a little time fussing with her hair before she had gathered enough strength to re-enter the arena. "Hi," said a short youth with horn-rimmed glasses that shielded him like a mask. "Hello, there," said Tanya and kept walking. "What do you do for a living?" he persisted, but she had turned the corner.

When you said good-by, love,
What had we to gain?
When I gave you my love
Was it all in vain?

There was an empty chair in the corner of the main room and she headed for it.

"Well, then, who *is* your idea of a beautiful woman?" asked a man in a red vest.

"Eleanor Roosevelt," a fat girl replied.

Someone was offering potato chips. A barefooted woman was demonstrating the twist to the wrong music. Tanya pinched each hip, hiked up her dress a quarter of an inch and sat down. She felt peacefully alone, her heavy unhappiness dormant and resting. She wondered if a miracle would happen and the whole evening pass without her having to say a single word.

"This is Dexter Morganstern," said Marcia's voice. Tanya looked up and found a man with a clean young face and tar-black hair who smiled a desperate message of admiration and subservience. Marcia vanished, and the young man sat on a footrest like a slave at Tanya's feet.

"I hope you don't mind?"

"Why should I mind?"

"I understand you're an actress."

"As luck would have it."

"Good for you. I once wanted to be an actor."

"Oh?"

"I have a great love tor the theater."

"Uh, huh."

They talked on and on and if, afterward, Tanya had tried to recall what exactly she had said she would not have been able to do so. Oh, kind sir. Sweet gentle boring sir, please leave me alone. Oh, gentle, clean-cut young man, instructor of English at some college or other upstate, why go through all this? It will gain thee not. She wished she were in bed with the covers over her. What? Yes, I think Gielgud is a fine actor. Yes, Julie Harris is fine, too. Who are my favorites? Joseph Weisman. You haven't heard of him? George C. Scott? Him neither? You really do love the theater, don't you? God, such a love for the theater.

"What were you in" he asked, smiling. "Perhaps I saw you?"

"*A TV show*. Murder on Fire Island."

"No, I'm afraid ... I'm sorry. What else?"

He was eager to have seen her in something, if only for her sake.

"A film called *Superego*. Soon to be released, as they say."

"Oh, good."

"Were you ever in St. Louis?"

"Why, yes, I was. Did you do something there?"

"I was in the pantomime theater."

His face fell. "It's a tough profession, acting." This, after an empty pause. "Like writing. As I said, I'm a teacher. I'm supposed to publish in my field. Which is literature. But I don't often. Not enough." He stalled, losing his point. "Do you know the joke about Christ? They're taking him down from the cross and someone says he's a teacher but..."

"Yes, I know that one."

"Oh, yes?"

"It's very funny."

"Yes."

He had lost and he knew it. "I like your dress."

"Do you? It's taffeta."

"You know something? You're very nice."

"Why, thank you."

Somehow she got away. Yet in whatever room she entered, Dexter What'shisname seemed to appear.

"What do you mean you're going to die young?" said the high blonde. "You're too old to die young."

The Scotch was going fast, and Tanya filled up in self-defense, noting that several men were maneuvering into position to talk to her. For protection, she began a conversation with a flat-faced woman in her forties, and they discussed the grandeur of the Mendelson apartment and the low rent. As they talked, Tanya kept saying, "No, I don't think so," or "No, not right now, thank you," to the five men who came up one by one and asked her to dance.

This love of mine
Goes on and on
Though life is empty
Since you have gone.

She wandered about some more (silently mouthing the lyrics), and entered a room where a pile of coats lay on the bed like a dead giant. She found herself alone. A pretty dark-haired girl with a bit of her bra showing frowned at herself from the mirror. She and the girl shouldered and fingered the bra in place, then the twins looked at each other, flexed a smile and released it. They made a series of absurd faces at each other. One was so odd, they broke into laughter over it. Two tongues were stuck out at each other, two eyes winked winsomely, and four full lips parted in mock seductiveness.

"You always make faces at yourself?"

Dexter What'shisname was in the doorway.

"Only when I'm alone," she replied with embarrassment.

"Well, bravo. I award you a standing ovation." And he approached, clapping.

This time, perhaps it was the liquor or catching her off guard, he had strength. He talked; he didn't question. He took the initiative and held it. The secret voice in him that had kept saying *I need you, I need you,* was gone. On the wall was a cartoon from *The New Yorker.* It showed a Christmas wreath hung on the door of a fallout shelter. This was the starting point of a discussion that included civil disobedience, underground testing, Linus Pauling, and Bertrand Russell. Tanya came alive. Here, talking to her, was a man who cared. He, too, was against building fallout shelters. He, too, had picketed for Negro rights. He, too, marched on Washington. She stood with her back to the mirror, drank, smoked, and listened.

Then Marcia came running in, pulling Irving by the hand. It was twelve midnight. Happy New Year. Whistles were blowing, people grew noisy. The Mendelsons kissed. Tanya looked at Dexter.

He only smiled. "Well," said she, "when in Rome dere do as the Rumanians do." The touch of his sharkskin suit. A wet kiss. The rapture of Old Spice.

The man in the red vest entered the room while they were still embracing. "We all admire the way you're fighting homosexuality," he said to Dexter.

Laughter all around. Tanya got a fatherly kiss from Irving. Red Vest, unsteady under the weight of six ounces of vodka, tried to sweep Tanya into his arms. Dexter handled the situation deftly. Val would never have come to her aid, she thought. He would have stood back chuckling over the amusing ways of man. The others drifted out but Tanya didn't want to leave the seclusion of the bedroom, and so Dexter went to refill their drinks, leaving her alone with the monster of coats, her mirrored twins, and Mr. Sinatra.

I get along without you very well.
Of course I do.
Except when soft rains fall
And drip from leaves
Then I recall…

She opened a door and stepped out onto a balcony. Her flesh shuddered with the cold. Above were delicate pinholes of light, and the distant windows were framed with colored bulbs. The first kiss is long remembered. His hand had cupped her head, still holding the scissors. His chuckling laughter afterward. Her broken bra, like the scales of justice, she kicked aside with her foot. She remembered well. The kiss she had just tasted was nothing like it.

Valitchska, you bastard. How she hated him! After that ruinous Christmas Eve she had emphatically returned one of his books in the mail. A note had gone with it asking him not to call anymore. So what did the bastard do? He did exactly what she asked. Not one call or protest or cry of pain. Seven days of silence and her life ran dry. So she kissed Dexter What'shisname but it tasted nothing like it.

I've forgotten you just like I should.
Of course I did.
Except to hear your name
Or someone's laugh that is the same.
But I've forgotten you just like I should.

The wind inflated her dress. A boat wailed a message of loss from a nearby river. A blanket was wrapped around her and she caught the smell of Old Spice again. His clean face and noble black hair remained beside her while the cold wind cut into her body and made her cry. For a while, however, she would not go indoors.

A girl whom Tanya had not recalled seeing before had passed out among the coats. Dexter was rummaging through the bookcase.

"Marcia says she has magazines with you in them. I wonder if one of these..."

"Oh, please don't," she said. "Let's join the others."

But he had taken up a copy of *Beauty and the Camera* and in no time had found her.

"Ah!" His eyes looked up at her and back to the page. "Say, this is all right. Marvelous." She joined him and looked at herself in flat black and white. The sea slapped at her jumping thighs as she beamed in acrobatic joy in a two-piece bathing suit, the very summation of beauty and youth. Except she had had her period that morning and the sea was icy cold in May. Recalling that the photos of her in this magazine weren't nudes, she relaxed and said, "Turn the page," and there she was again with elongated legs on a soft couch in a new yellow negligee that came out pure white. Her image presented an eager expression of acute longing though she had been eight days overdue at the time and beside herself with worry.

He said all the polite, sincere, and appropriate things; then he read the captions and asked who De Franco was.

"He's the photographer."

"But I mean who is he, someone important? In his field, that is?"

"Once he was almost famous."

He smiled, suspecting a joke. "How do you mean, almost famous?"

"Oh, it's a long story," she said, wearily lifting her empty paper cup to her lips. "He simply throws away his talent every chance he gets." Then she added: "Why don't we go in and join the others."

"Why does he throw it away?"

"I wish I knew. Come on, let's go."

"How well do you know him? Or am I asking a personal question?"

"You're not, no. I know him, let's see, for a year I guess. A little less."

"Oh, I see."

"Well, so that's it. Shall we go inside?"

"When a man throws away a talent like that, it makes me feel sick. I'd give so much to be really talented."

"I'm going inside," she said.

He walked with her toward the door. "You know, I wish this next year would pass in five seconds."

"Why?"

"Then it would be midnight once more and I could kiss you again." She smiled.

"Tanya, you look very lovely. You do."

"Gracias."

Stepping closer. "May I? Please?"

"I don't..."

"Just..."

"Stop, *stop!*"

"All right, sure," he said, frightened by the tone of her voice.

"I'm going to the ladies' room."

"You're not angry?"

"I'm not angry."

"I'll wait for you in ... "

She closed, locked, and leaned against the door, her face pressed into a dangling towel of rough cloth. High heels sounded on the other side. A hand rattled the knob. Gone. Silence except for

Always get that mood indigo
Since my baby said goodbye.
In the evening when the lights are low
I'm so lonely I could cry.

She flipped the top down on the toilet seat and perched upon it like a child in a bus terminal waiting to be found. Her cup stood on the enameled tomb of the tub. It occurred to her that a white, antiseptic bathroom was the perfect chamber in which to suffer. Here one could not lie down in green pastures. Here one was truly upright and alone. I am unhappy, her lips said, but there was no one to read them. She placed her hand on the cold sink and leaned her head down, the tears seeping through her closed lids.

Summer rubbed itself against her bare midriff as she stood by the open window above a tree and a triangle of earth. Ice cream! She didn't dare go down to buy some for she would miss the phone when it rang, if it rang. Wearing green slacks and a halter, she moved aimlessly about the room suddenly performing a few steps of a vaudeville routine (with invisible hat and cane) and then discovered Other Cat on the dining table and pushed him off. Seated in the couch, she read a few paragraphs of *Act One* by Moss Hart which sent her wandering off to a Brooklyn public school auditorium where, at twelve, she had given her first stage performance: a high-pitched Pocahontas opposite a pimply John Smith. Afterward everyone congratulated Emma Kretchmar except her mother who that evening began applying bleach to her daughter's skin so she would look less like a wop.

The first ring gave her a near-fatal jolt. *Act One* fell and lost its dust jacket and place mark. An ashtray spilled, one slipper came off, and she tripped on the rug before she finally got her fingers on the phone. She waited, however, until the second ring was completed before lifting the receiver. It was the wrong number. To abate a feeling of letdown, she spoke to Tom Tom, who was sniffing among the spilt ashes on the rug. "He vonted Gustov. I told'm dere ist no Gustov." She turned the radio on and scraped up the ashes only to spill them once more on her second rush for the phone. Another request for Gustov. She stood by the window again with Other Cat rubbing against her stomach. A man was lobbing slices of bread from his window into the courtyard. Tanya stroked the animal and stared at the tree, unable to read its message of form and silence. A piece of stale pumpernickel was caught in its branches.

Back to the couch to do more reading. She glanced at the black phone. Call, you bastard. Another cigarette lit and burning. More words from Moss Hart. Again the phone rang. Her number had been selected by the Fred Astaire Dance Studio; a professional lesson was hers free of charge with no obligations. Tanya hung up, head shaking. "At least it wasn't Gustov asking if there were any messages." A noise in the bedroom told her that Cat was on the dresser. She went in and dumped the animal to the floor and righted a bottle of Shalimar by Guerlain. She opened it and dabbed herself behind both ears. A drop for the bazooms.

Back in the living room, she realized that it was a while now since she had turned on the radio. It had remained dead, the plug pulled out during housecleaning. Soon she was swimming through Rachmaninoff's "Third Piano Concerto," seated in her Carole Lombard chair and lost in the taxing preoccupation of being Van Cliburn. Supreme at her invisible piano, she rested patiently while the orchestra strode on alone. Then she would come in with soft fingers, or hands pounding, her face revealing the various moods of the poetic soul.

Elated, her fingers exhausted, she stood and bowed to crashing applause. A huge concert hall was acclaiming her with tumultuous love. She bowed again and again, accepting the triumph with a slight grin. An astonishing debut, heralding an immortal career; Tanya Lando known and adored by all.

The mundane voice of the announcer shattered the spell. Tanya fed the cats and started dinner. Knowing that phones always ring when people take showers, she took a shower but the phone didn't ring. In a housecoat, she came out and studied the living-room clock. Five after six. All was lost. Mike closes his office at five thirty

Saturday and then drives to Fire Island. Was there then to be no part, no play, no career?

The downstairs buzzer sounded like the ten-second warning at Madison Square Garden and, hating electronics, she pressed the button with an angry jab. Leaving the door ajar, she went back to the kitchen. A cautious hello preceded him into the apartment and there was Dexter Morganstern with a bottle of wine in a paper bag. Holding her housecoat closed with one hand, she brought out the spaghetti and then the lamb chops and then scooted next door to borrow a corkscrew. When she came back, he said that she had gotten a call from a Mike Ferrero who wanted her to ring him back right away. It had something to do with an off-Broadway production of *The Idiot.* Tanya pounced on the phone, misdialed, began again, got a busy signal, and screamed. She tried once more, and again it was busy. She brought out the garlic bread and tried again. She brought out the salad and tried a fourth time. She sat down across from him at the table. Got up to get the salt. Sat down. Got up to dial. Sat down. Got up for the grated cheese. Dialed once more. Sat down. Ate some spaghetti, sipped some wine, tasted neither, shouted, "I can't stand it," and collapsed on the phone once again. Then, to the ceiling, she said: "Thank God, it's ringing."

Her guest viewed all this with puzzled amusement, hungrily eating the food and tasting the wine, while Tanya said: "Hi, there. Any news?" She knelt, her shoulders crouched as though expecting a blow, her free hand held high, fingers crossed. "Yeh," she said and paused. "Yeh." Silence. Then an explosion. She screamed and danced, yelled and jumped, kissed him, kissed the phone, kissed the cats and collapsed grinning into a chair, vindicated and victorious.

He seemed somewhat detached from her manic celebration. The way her housecoat had parted during the excitement, the way it now hung open as she sagged limply with both knees over the arm of the easy chair, her long permanently tanned legs uncovered and warm with passive invitation, all this seemed to make him aware of another victory, one that he, too, had long wanted and as yet had been denied.

"Hy am Nastasya Filippovna," Tanya announced, when she had returned to the table. "Hy am a great Russian vumman vid passion and desire. Hy am beink beautiful and hy am drivink men mad."

She turned adolescent with delight. He said he was happy for her, pointing out, however, that the food was getting cold. Tanya eventually finished the meal, but only with his constant prodding. To everyone she could think of who had anything to do with her getting the role, she lifted her glass in salute. She even drank a toast to next Monday afternoon, the appointed time for the signing of the contract. Her joy was unmanageable and kept returning anew. She rejected dessert, and perched herself on his lap to recite for him passages from the play. Later, when her delight had leveled off and with the red spot of her cigarette deepening in the all but total darkness, his disembodied voice, out of tune with the drifting summer mood, asked her if she would please sleep with him.

He was like an anecdoteless saint or the friend one remembers fondly, yet rarely visits. He was not dull, just lacking. Not weak, simply doting. All and all, totally damned with virtues. He was permanently inflicted with that faultless diplomacy that always charms those who meet him yet which leaves afterwards a blank in their memories. Tanya was pleased by his glossy good looks and his expression of profound innocence and sobriety. He was dedicated, considerate, and loving, and this bothered her. For six months now she had adopted a world-weary abstinence, and he was so dedicated, considerate, and loving that he had allowed her to get away with it.

Yet she believed a new day of enlightenment for her was dawning and, re-enforced by her elation, she decided to throw away her old neurotic patterns and to try to stick it out with someone who was not, from the very start, all wrong. She killed her cigarette while a column of cool evening air moved between their faces. The room had lost dimension, and she could see only the barest caricature of his face, still sober, patiently awaiting the answer to his question.

With the sound of one of the cats ferreting about in a corner, she undid two buttons on his shirt and pressed her hand against the undergrowth of his chest. She pushed a series of lightweight kisses against his shave-lotioned face as though languidly drawing sustenance from his mouth. When she felt his arms tightening, she asked him instead to go with her into the bedroom, which they did carrying glasses of whiskey and ice. As the darkness faded slightly, she saw him folding his pants over a chair as though he were involved in an act of meticulous measurement. He approached with meek hands to explore her summer's flesh, disappointing her with his reverence. That never-quite-knowing newness of someone else for the first time. Suddenly a neighbor's window spilled pale light across her sculpturesque stomach and his harsh hip. The reclining completeness of her seemed to inflict him with hesitation and awe. The abrupt weight of a cat on the bed brought forth her bare foot, searching, finding fur and pushing it off. Then to her yielding regret, he was in her too soon, riding but getting her nowhere, just losing himself in his private lunacy. They were like two innocent children marching out of step, and she tried all she could to summon up her lust. Then, just as she was discovering thin fabrics of pleasure, creating constrictions of desire, he went through the happy, brief shuddering of a petit mal, and it was over.

It had begun like everything in her life: badly. But she was not really concerned. Reassuring him that it was all right, she sipped her drink, stared into the dark, and waited for the coils of her lust to cool down. He remained distraught, and to express her fondness and to shelter his little boy's fear, she rolled into his arms and made the irresponsible assertion that she loved him. She didn't remember falling asleep, only coming awake with him asleep beside her in the quiet room. At that moment, the phone jarred her.

She fumbled in darkness, struggled with the wire, engineered the receiver to her ear, and knocked over her drink.

"Ah, *shit*. It spilt ... Hello?"

"Hello."

"Damn, it's over everything."

"What is?"

"I knocked over a drink. Tsh. Wait a minute. Hang on. Oi vay."

INTERVIEW

*T**ANYA LANDO is a tall, attractive young actress destined perhaps for stardom. She took the first big step in this direction when she recently won the lead in Maxwell Sherwood's off-Broadway production of The Idiot by Dostoevsky. She has a soulful, playful, intent, intelligent face framed by black hair parted in the center and touching her shoulders; she has a slim yet full figure referred to not inaccurately in her press release as "sensational," and she has long, shapely legs which her agent terms "second to none." This afternoon, she is wearing what she herself calls her Freud-red dress.*

Seated in a canvas chair which once belonged to Carole Lombard and whose name is still printed on the back, Miss Lando does a mock imitation of a kittenish little girl about to take an examination and trying to win over the examiner. Hands folded in her lap, knees and ankles together, she is the picture of nervous, flirtatious expectancy. Soon, though, she leans back, arms and hands lifting to the wooden armrests; her left knee slowly rises as if without her knowledge or as though trying not to attract attention, and gradually, gracefully she crosses her legs. Now her knee is fully showing but there is no cover-up tug with her dress. Before long she is wiggling her foot, gesturing, frowning, laughing. Not a controlled, vacuous, self-conscious starlet but a responding, intelligent, independent woman.

In the living room of her apartment, which she shares with another actress, and which she says is decorated in "Presbyterian Baroque" there is hung on the walls: a bullfight poster (Dominguin, Litri, Arutha), an Air France travel poster on Italy, a straw Christ on a straw cross, a reproduction of Modigliani's "Head of a Woman," a postcard showing a painting by Orozco, an African mask, a framed photograph showing Tanya with Jerry Lester on one side and Joey Adams on the other, a Mexican blanket, a thermometer, and a faked newspaper headline reading tanya lando renounces group therapy. tshombe stunned.

Among her records we spotted ten albums of Broadway musicals, two records by Cal Orff, a Vox Box of Vivaldi, "The Cantata for the Sixteeth Sunday After Trinity" by Bach and five LP's of Frank Sinatra. Her library, on three shelves of bricks and boards, was made up almost entirely of plays and play anthologies. Above the bookcase is a large tank of greenish water. Swimming inside were Fish, Other Fish, Finch, and Tuna Finch. Two turtles were Quemoy and Matsu. The Angora, Siamese, and tomcat are called, respectively, Cat, Other Cat, and Tom Tom. The two canaries in a cage by the window are Fifth Amendment and Eileen Herlie. Tanya's roommate is Silvia Brown (away at summer stock) and Tanya's real name is Emma Kretchmar.

TANYA: Isn't that the worst? You could choke on your matzo with a name like that. I tell my mother I went into show business just so I could change it.

INTERVIEWER: How did your mother respond to your entering the business?

TANYA: You know the joke. She was wonderful when I told her over the phone. She had heard about the casting couch and the wild parties and how everyone marries and divorces everyone else, but she said as long as it was what I wanted and I was happy. I said, "Momma, how come you're taking it so well?" and she said, "So vy shouldn't I take it vell? Besides, as soon as I'm hanging up, I'm killing myself."

INTERVIEWER: Doesn't she take pleasure from your successes?

TANYA: Successes is like not what she would call them. Let me see, I was Miss Dairy Queen, Miss Donut Queen, Miss Smooth Skin, Miss Fishing Tackle, Miss Wesport, Miss Independence Day 1959, Miss Sweater Girl 1957, Miss Best Legs, Miss Virginia Beach, Miss Best Posture, Miss Ring-a-Ding-Ding and once I was the Playboy

INTERVIEWER: Playmate for June. Thrilled, my mother wasn't. I understand that if you succeed in *The Idiot* then United Artists wants to give you a screen test.

TANYA: What they don't remember is they already gave me one four years ago. I was so bad they had to reshoot the thing before they could throw it out. I played a jungle girl dressed in a leopard Bikini plus pancake makeup, mascara, and false eyelashes. Dying of invisible gunshot wounds, I did a Camille death scene clasped in my lover's arms, and for the first three takes I just kept cracking up. It was kind of comical-tragical if you know what I mean. Too much, I tell you, too much.

INTERVIEWER: But you did get to make some films, I understand.

TANYA: Two, actually. One was a short experimental thing with dream sequences, blurred focusing —the works. It was, what's the word? cryptic. Real cryptic. And tedious, wow. It was done by an amateur group on Long Island. It was, *como se dice?* meaningful. I played a psychotic schizophrenic who was an ex-stripper. It wasn't easy. It all takes place in a nut house, and I did this mad, surrealistic strip. It was called *Superego.* Cinema 16 showed it once and (could you believe it?) I actually got a few job offers here and there because of that little film. I was amazed. The other was just a walk-on out in Hollywood. I strode up to Bob Mitchum in a nightclub and sold him a pack of cigarettes. A great demand for me, because of this part, there wasn't.

INTERVIEWER: What events led up to your winning the role of Nastasya Filippovna in *The Idiot?*

TANYA: Again it was by taking my clothes off. Professionally speaking, of course. Of course. I was on a TV mystery drama called *Murder on Fire Island*. A heartwarming tale of sex and death. I played the whole thing in a two-piece bathing suit. Well, Jonathan Cobb saw it and that led to a tryout. I competed with six other girls for the part. Some of them had much bigger names. I died. I never thought I'd get it. Never. There was a month of tryouts and eliminations. How I lived through that month, like I'll never know. But I guess all good things come from taking your clothes off. See how a girl gets conditioned. Anyway, I got the part and just under the wire, too.

INTERVIEWER: What do you mean, just under the wire?

TANYA: Well, some years ago I gave myself until I was twentynine to—you know—makeah ze big splash. That deadline still holds. I'm twenty-eight and many, many months. I don't think I'm supposed to tell you that. Mike—my agent Mike Ferraro—will have a fit. All starlets are supposed to be twenty-one until they drop. It's not easy. The first thing I do when I get thirty is demand a recount.

INTERVIEWER: You look at most twenty-four, twenty-five tops.

TANYA: Bless you. Well, actually, people have said that. They had better say that. My agent wants me to tell the press that it's due to milk baths and yoga but who can practice yoga in a tub of milk? My analyst says it's due to living for years on a neurotically surface personality. What the hell, as long as you've got your health.

INTERVIEWER: Describe a typical day in the life of Tanya Lando.

TANYA: My usual day is one of anguish offset by confusion and relieved by moments of acid indigestion.

INTERVIEWER: What do you do from the moment you get up?

TANYA: *(very quickly)* Up at eight. Exercise. Quick breakfast. Yogurt and fruit. Then acting classes, dancing classes, singing classes, elocution classes. *Lunch!* Fruit and yogurt. More classes. Studying, doing tryouts, making calls. *Dinner!* Yogurt and one *egg.* Medium rare. No fruit. Studying, reading, no dates, early to bed. *Morning!* Up at eight. Who-ha. And if you believe that, lots of luck.

INTERVIEWER: No social life at all?

TANYA: I knew you'd get to that one. What is the standard reply? But darlink, kai don't have time for men. For diamonds, yes, but for men.... Well, there'll be a book written about me someday, and it'll be called *The Men in Her Life and Other Kinds of Tzurus.* My analyst says I get involved in dead-end social relationships because I don't really want to get married due to a subconscious fear of my father. It's not easy. A phone call, a quiet dinner for two. God, the miseries that can lead to! But it must be true what my analyst says 'cause here I sit single as all hell and with all my friends getting married for the second time. Think of all the money I blow on wedding gifts.

INTERVIEWER: Your agent says you have strong opinions. He says you're a member of SANE, that you've picketed the UN, that you've marched on Washington and that he had all he could do to keep you from going on a freedom ride.

TANYA: Mike told you that? Honorable agent has rotund mouth. You have a cigarette? I'm all out. Crazy. Thanks. *(Recrossing her legs, this time fast, decisive.)* What can I say about Mike's politics? Mike's up to his neck in business, and he doesn't really want to make waves. I love him as an agent and as a man. But politically like he stands about 1890. We have lovely discussions about world affairs. We check our guns at the door. We even check the door. *Mamma mia.* Once I nearly threw a vase at him. I didn't though. It was my vase. These are perilous times, Oh. let's not get on politics. Let's go back to taking off clothes. In fact, what time is it? Hey, I've got a rehearsal.

INTERVIEWER: Then one more question and you'll just love this one. Miss Lando, what is it you want out of life?

TANYA: Phew! Yeh. Well, what are you going to do? O.K., what do I want? Vell, havant Halizabeth Taylor, she should find heppiness. Like is that so much to hask? And havant there shouldn't be ha vor. No fighting. Havant Jonathan Vinters, that nice man, he should find himself ha show on Broadvay. And in da bones dere, no Stronsom 90.

INTERVIEWER: But for yourself? What do you want?

TANYA: For me? Oh, I don't know. Moneypowerglory plus, oh, plus a man, a career, a feeling of worthiness, of usefulness. And since you can't live forever, a sense, a definite sense of progress. Sorry I can't be more profound.

INTERVIEWER: Progress within yourself?

TANYA: In everything. In people. In government. In art. You know, like progress.

INTERVIEWER: Thank you, Miss Lando.

TANYA: Thank *you*. Really, thanks. Tvus ha great sperchul hacksppearance.

THE instant Val emerged from the poplars, he saw it lying there unguarded on a white towel. Carrying a shoe on each thumb, he trudged through yielding sand to where black water lapped timidly against a formation of rock. Two distant sun-worshipers lay face down on a blanket as though they had been struck on the head from behind. Val removed his white navy pants and black shirt (tails knotted in front to form a bare midriff) and left them on the rock. He walked back in his bathing suit, oblivious to stones beneath his feet. The distant couple remained motionless, heads still turned away. He waited a moment, then dropped to a crouch, his xylophone ribs moving gently. Across the towel THE GUARDIAN COUNTRY CLUB was printed in red.

There was no dent in the milled wheel, and he didn't check for an ink stain on the strap since there was neither strap nor case. A lake breeze licked his skin. As with the stones, he took no notice. He was transfixed by the beauty of it as it lay on the towel. He eyed its shape and functional parts in a way that no man could unless he had once owned one and then did so no longer. Two large vacant blue eyes, one above the other, stared at him, and he could feel the black corrugated surface without touching it. He looked around quickly, then reached out and took it into his hands. It was like finding an ice skate in the middle of a jungle.

After a few moments he placed the Rolleiflex back on the towel, this time with the lens away from the sun. He walked with discomfort across the jagged sand and into the lake, the slime sucking at his feet as the water rose to his knees. He pitched forward with a smile, feeling very cold then, after a few strokes, not cold at all as he caught a glimpse of the motionless float toward which he strove. Standing upon it with his back to the shore he felt cold again, though it was the new and tremendous excitement in him and not the chills that pushed his feet into a little dance and sent him diving once more into the lake. He swam down into the pressing silence until the morning almost flickered out above him, giving way to the intimidating darkness below. Then he made the final decision: yes, he would try to steal it. Exhilarated, he headed back and swam into the sky. On the float again, he lay with his back on the separated planks of wood but didn't look to the shore. I'll count to a thousand, he thought, and then if the son-of-a-bitch who owns it doesn't come back I'll grab it. As he reached four hundred, waves from a passing motorboat nudged the raft like a cradle. At six hundred he closed his eyes and folded his hands behind his head. His face was narrow and lean like an unsuccessful caricature with no single feature dominating. This was the feeling the bartender had had the night before when Val entered the saloon in Monticello, holding his camera by the strap like a rabbit by its ears and, placing it on the bar, said, "Johnnie Walker Black."

He had the habit of coming into a room talking, whether he knew a soul in the place or not. He could melt austerity with a sentence, almost any sentence ("My, *you're* looking happy" or "Now, there *is* a good-looking jacket") and within minutes the people in the bar had grown immeasurably friendlier to him and to each other. Having been asked the question, he assured them he wasn't an actor. "I'm rarely even an *audience*."

A caravan of film people had recently arrived from Hollywood to shoot a B picture about summer life in the "Borscht Belt." Reports persisted of movie stars having been seen here or there around town, so that whenever anyone new appeared he was given a quick once-over.

Actually, the contest started quite by accident. As Val disappeared from the sight of those standing at the bar to remove his shoes because they were hurting his feet, he overheard someone insist that a man who could finish a fifth of booze and remain on his feet wasn't so much a good drinker as he was a good eater. Val stood up an inch shorter and pushing his hair from his face replied that he knew of someone who could stay on his feet after finishing a fifth and who didn't need the aid of a full stomach at all. A polite Canadian with the smile of a retired gambler placed his hand on Val's shoulder to say that he had often heard of those so-called great drinkers. Never, though, in all his fifty-nine years had he ever met or even learned the name of one.

"Well," said Val, "the guy who finished that fifth on an empty stomach was named De Franco."

"And who may he be?" asked the other, like a lawyer moving in on a piece of flimsy evidence.

"Oh, some mad rogue."

"Well, where might he be?"

"A step closer, for Christ sake, and you'd be hugging 'im."

"Ah, Mr. De Franco. Well, I suppose you just finished a seven-course meal and it wouldn't be fair to demonstrate now on my money."

"I had one sandwich an hour ago and on *your* money, I'll demonstrate anything."

They put a bottle of Johnnie Walker in front of him, filled his shot glass, placed it beside his camera and checked the time. It was 8:18. By 10:12 the bottle was empty, and Val, holding the last of the Scotch in his little glass was saying: "Now I can either talk this way or cy con falk sis fay. But either way you must admit I'm *def*initely on my feet." With a cryptic laugh he downed the last of the whiskey to prompt applause.

Waving good-by, he left, returned to put on his shoes, and left again. He moved through dark Monticello streets having stepped into a world seething with significance and beyond comprehension. There was a noise as though the universe was breathing one mighty, everlasting intake of air, and it seemed that the laws of nature had been changed so that one moved suddenly, if one moved at all. When he spotted a cat under a streetlight hunched upon a mailbox, he photographed it to see if the picture would look as marvelous sober as the reality looked while drunk. Then noticing a small park, he wandered in and knelt as soon as he found grass. Flinging out both arms (one hand still holding the camera like a rabbit by its ears) he stared at the electric bulb moon with an ecstatic grin before hitting the lawn with his face.

He was dry by the time he had counted to a thousand. For good measure he counted five hundred more, and by that time even his suit was dry. He stood on the float and saw, on one of the green planks beneath his bare feet, the words DON'T PUSH OR ROCK printed in neat white letters. He dove and swam for shore and came out a dozen feet or so from where he first went in. Near the sunbathers, who hadn't stirred, was a little dog sniffing about. Far out in the lake a water skier followed behind a speedboat with monotonous immobility. Val walked through the yielding sand to the white towel that said THE GUARDIAN COUNTRY CLUB. The camera was gone. With a snap of his fingers he turned and went back to where he had left his clothes, and they too were gone. Rhythms of water snickered against the rock. The sunbathers still bathed, the dog still prowled, and on the lake the skier, like some amphibious equestrian who had lost his horse, still hurried along clutching the reins of the runaway boat as though for his very life. Val laughed at himself. "Of course," he cried aloud, shutting his eyes and tilting his head, transforming the pain into a kind of comic inevitability. "Of course." He sobered, shook his head, sucked his teeth, and said, "Screw 'em," and went back for a swim.

Honey appeared at the crossing carrying the traditional hatbox which contained the things he had told her to bring: her new Bikini, a change of sweater and skirt, the toreador pants that fitted her so well, two pairs of spiked shoes, a very old leotard, and a pair of net stockings. She wore a simple flared skirt, a blouse, and leather sandals. Yet her blond hair had been worked on carefully and her eyes were deeply accented with theatrical makeup.

Though she was forty minutes late there was no one in sight, and so, mouthing an ice cream cone, she waited in the shade upon a rail fence beneath a large oak. A twig fell and flicked her on the head. She smoothed her hair and checked her palm. Another twig fell and again she touched her head. The third time, she looked up as though to scold nature itself.

"I thought there was somethin' fishy," she said, stepping back, beaming at the sight of him among the branches.

In a brown suit, dated by its large lapels and pleated pants, which he had owned for ten years and hadn't worn in three, Val climbed down.

"No pictures today," he explained. "Would have saved you the trip but I didn't know where to get in *touch* with you, you *mystery* woman."

"Why? Anything wrong?"

"I passed out last night after a bit of drinking. When I awoke, the strap was still in my hand but some son-of-a-bitch had cut away the camera with a knife."

Honey gasped and then did it again when Val said his wallet had been taken as well.

"And this morning by the lake they took my clothes," said Val. "I'm so glad I travel light. Tomorrow I'll probably *vanish* completely. That's why I'm wearing this *winged* buzzard," he added, flipping forward the lapels with his thumbs. "Lucky I brought it along. What it really needs is a visor and shield."

They chose a path that turned into the woods so they could escape the haze that was lifted whenever a car passed. The heat was growing intense, and Val removed his jacket, letting it drape from a finger over his back. A couple of thorns were clinging to his pants below the side pocket. The blonde licked the last of the moisture from her cone and tossed it uneaten against the bark of a tree. A spell of intense thought had given her face an expression of mourning. She opened the hatbox, fumbled for and found what she wanted. She held out her fist, and as he finished the story of how he had nearly robbed some bastard of a camera down at the lake, he placed his left palm beneath her hand, expecting for some reason the gift of a piece of candy but he found instead two ten-dollar bills crumpled up like bits of trash in his hand.

And the first time he had ever seen her was just twenty-four hours before. Seven photographers were seated on the same side of a parked studio truck, three on the running board and two on each fender. They were facing a uniformed guard standing at a gate behind which there was a graveled road that led to one of the private beaches of the Guardian Country Club which the management had allowed Metro-Goldwyn-Mayer to use that afternoon to shoot a scene. The trouble was that the director of the film had suddenly reversed his usual policy of allowing photographers on location, and they were now eating their lunch and bitching about their bad luck as they sat facing the gate through which they were unable to pass.

Seated on the running board, Val unwrapped a tuna fish sandwich on the lap of his white sailor pants as he listened with amusement to the general murmur of complaints. Most of the men left soon after lunch. Some tried just once more to argue their way through the gate before giving up and heading back to New York or Boston; others decided to make the best of what was left of a sunny day by returning to their hotel and using the pool.

Val remained alone on the running board dreaming in the sun. Reaching into his gadget bag, he removed a peach, and leaning away from himself, took a wet bite. He sat back, his eyes closed, his face toward the light, humming a theme whose composer, he suspected, was Prokofiev. He listened to the birds for a while and then hummed the theme once more.

"D'ya know what time it is?"

She was standing close to him and blocking out the sun. A chin-high choker of rhinestones and pearls, with earrings to match, set her neck and ears sparkling, and she wore a marvelous, large-brimmed blue hat. In contrast to a whisper of pale lipstick was the delicacy of black magic with which she had landscaped her eyes. A dark, strapless gown with matching gloves finished the job and left as a feast for the eye the uninterrupted curves of neck, of shoulders, of bold, peek-a-boo breasts. He felt he could hardly see her at all, protected as she was by the armor plating of all this glamour.

"I don't carry a watch," he said, "but it's Tuesday... I *think*."

She seemed a bit lost for a moment as she glanced about her. Then she smiled at him as though, if she had her way, many more of the young men of the world would look like this one and would even sit on running boards of parked trucks with their shirts open, humming away happily and holding a half-eaten peach.

"Funny, I thought it was Wednesday," she said.

"Where'd you just come from? Did you *spring* out of the earth?"

"Through that gate. I thought there'd be others here. I'm lookin' for a photo-grapher. I was supposed to sign a what-do-ya-call-it for him?"

"A release," he said, trying to hold back a smile.

"That's it, sign a release."

Glancing about again, she tilted her head to feel if her hair was still up in back.

"Well, they all left. Maybe you can catch up with them."

He pointed down the road where a sparrow pecked at a puddle and flew off in a blur.

"Well, what's *your* name?" she asked, blinking at him with eyes of calculating innocence. When he told her, she said with moderate excitement:

"I've seen your work."

"Then you've been reading trashy magazines, young lady."

"You know something, you look like a young John Carradine, you really do. And that peach, I bet it tastes good."

"Have a bite."

Not touching it with her hands, baring her teeth so as not to smudge her lips, she leaned over and bit into the fruit while he, looking down into her dress, entertained himself with an aerial view of her lovely melons.

"You in the film?" he asked, nodding toward the gate where the guard had taken his eyes off the blonde for a moment to slap his neck.

"It's not exactly a juicy part," she answered, her words wet from the peach. "I'm only a starlet. But I have this scene with Mickey Rooney where I get my clothes torn off and they throw me in the lake. It's a wonderful opportunity for acting."

"What's the reason?" Val asked, tossing the pit into the grass.

"'Cause I get to make all kinds of faces and I get to scream, too."

"No, I mean what's the reason for throwing you in the lake?"

"'Cause the director says it's better than the way the script was written. These gangsters mistake me for Mickey Rooney's girl friend and threaten me with death if Mickey doesn't pay the ten thousand. But the director says this isn't human enough, so he also has 'em tear off my clothes and throw me in the lake."

Eyeing the guard, she made a face. "I hate cops. Can we walk?"

With his gadget bag on his shoulder and wiggling several fingers, sticky from the peach, he followed their shadows along a road that led through a camouflage of trees to the hotel.

"Christ, listen to that," Val exclaimed and imitated the bird call they had just heard.

"Oh, it's so lovely out here," said the blonde.

A station wagon came heading up the dirt road toward the gate. The starlet waved as the car passed, but no one waved back.

"They're in the film, too," she said.

The car had kept going, and Val decided not to wait any longer.

"I'm also a free-lance photographer," he said, slipping into his usual approach, "and I'd like to do a picture story on you for magazine publication. It'll be the usual stuff. Glamour, leg shots, and so forth. I would like ..."

"That sounds like fun." Her agreement took him by surprise. "Where will we do it? And what will I wear?"

It had been too easy. No look of suspicion, no request that he see her agent first, or that he name the magazine in which the pictures would appear. All this didn't fit in with what he knew to be the policy of agents and film companies to control such publicity.

"Take this road and meet me tomorrow at noon at the crossroads on the other side of that hill." Then, to decide once and for all whether she was as willing as she seemed: "We'll follow one of those footpaths and do the shooting somewhere in the woods."

The starlet held her hat on against a gust of wind, and pushed her dress back down over her dark nylons.

"Takin' pictures in the woods!" There was an emphatic alteration in her voice. "Why, that really sounds like fun, Mr. De Franco."

"I can see you're going to be no trouble at *all*," said Val, bubbling with optimism.

"Why, Mr. De Franco, how can you even think of such a thing?" she retorted with a coyness that didn't go with the elegance of her dress. "Li'l ol' me wouldn't make trouble."

"Well, until you *do*, you can call me Val." With each word stressed, he trembled with energy, his eyes popping. "Now what do *I* call you? What's *your* li'l ol' name?"

"I have a number of them. Which do you wanna use?"

"Oh, I don't know," said Val, completely charmed by her. "Which do you *suggest*?"

"I suggest you use my favorite."

"I'm with you, honey."

"Why, it just so happens…"

Above the clearing and below a migration of small, peaceful clouds, there tugged and pulled against an invisible string a tiny colorless kite. Now and then, when its tail went into a dither as though trying to get free and fly west, Val found himself hoping for the string to break. Seated on a log, he crossed his legs, tucked his shoe behind his shank, pulled a reed from the earth, started to speak, and was interrupted.

"What's the matter, aren't you trustworthy or somethin'? Don't worry. You'll pay me back. No more about it now, hear?"

"Where is it written, little girl, that I have to accept a loan?"

"Don't interrupt," said Honey Bea, "I'm thinkin' ."

"About the *money*, I hope," said Val, "'cause you may never see it again."

"Hush, now, I'm thinkin'."

Her hatbox, with its many changes of dress, lay unused in the high weeds as she stood frowning and biting a fingernail, the edges of her loose white skirt undulating in rhythm with the wind. There was almost no sign of the triumphant clotheshorse he had seen twenty-four hours earlier. She was hatless; her blond hair casually unkempt and with heavy makeup (the only carryover from the day before), she looked the part, in her low-cut blouse, of a determined Hollywood farm girl about to defend her honor against a villain in the wicked woods.

Val's body shook in silent merriment, the sloping reed quivering in his mouth. Unfolding the two crumpled bills in the palm of his hand, he laid them Hamilton side up and looked at them solemnly. "But she doesn't even *know* me," he said, as though she weren't standing right there, her ankles and sandals hidden by the grass. "She's just a crazy kook throwing away her hard-earned..."

"I got it!" She turned and faced him. "Can you meet me tonight in the lobby of the Guardian? About ten o'clock."

'Sure, but..."

"I should have it by then."

"*Have what*, for Christ sake?"

"A camera for you."

"What is this, *Christmas?*"

"You use one of them black square ones, don't you? What's it called?"

"Rolleiflex. Or a Rolleicord is good, too. In fact, any reflex that uses one-twenty..."

"Don't confuse me." She frowned her memory into action. "Rollei-flex, Rollei-cord," she said, chopping the air with her hand and repeating the names with rhythmic concentration.

"You mean to say you can get somebody to *lend* you a camera?"

"I think so." She was still frowning; the names of cameras tumbling through her head.

"If you can swing it, we could do the shooting tomorrow."

"That would be nice," she beamed, putting aside her memory lesson to tease him a little. "You sure you don't need nothin' else, now? Shirt? Socks? Everything you need you got. Is that right? You sure must love to give your belongings away. Like some kinda saint or somethin'."

"Looks that way, don't it?"

"Well, I think every man should have a hobby. Don't you?"

He gave several perplexed nods as though accepting a sudden revelation. "I take it all back. I see you're going to be trouble after all. Yes, I'm *sure* of it."

The wall was there to keep people out, and the vines that climbed the brick were too young to support a man's weight. Besides, a row of moonlit spikes could be clearly seen along the top. At the gate stood a uniformed guard cracking his knuckles.

"A lady is waiting inside for me," Val said.

"Can't letcha in," groaned a foghorn voice.

Val wanted to know why.

"Against regulations, Jack."

After a brief discussion, it was recommended that Val try the main gate down the road. Following the spiked wall, Val passed beneath an awning of trees blocking out the moon, and for a moment everything went black. The main gate was well lit, and this time there were two guards to talk with, but the answer was still the same, and Val grew angry. In their booth by the gate there was a phone. All he wanted them to do was lift the goddamn thing off the hook and call the lobby. Honey was probably waiting for him just yards from the switchboard. Again they said no. The only way to call the hotel, he was told, was to go back to town and phone from there. But the bus back would take half an hour and he was late already. The men would not give ground. They stood like trained apes, oblivious to reason.

Val marched back to the rear gate as though going to war. There, it would be man to man, one to one, and all he could think of on his way along the wall was the girl waiting in the lobby since ten o'clock. It was now ten twenty.

The man with the knuckles and the foghorn watched Val coming. About forty years old and too overweight to look good in uniform, he had the expression of a judge who condemned without evidence, of an executioner who throws the switch on your last words of prayer. The idea of trying a bribe had occurred to Val, but now his only wish was for justice.

"I'm going in," he said. "If you want to escort me to make sure I leave after I locate her, that's fine. But I'm going in with or without your permission, and I'm going in now."

Knuckles didn't move. Caution formed a half squint in the tail of his eyes. Val walked through the gate. The guard came running from behind and planted himself in Val's path. He seemed to be stalling. As Val walked around him, Knuckles reached out, and Val spun around.

"Don't touch me," he steamed. "Get one thing straight. Hands off."

Knuckles took a respectful step rearward. The matter seemed settled, and Val was about to proceed when the guard put a whistle to his lips and puffed out his cheeks in a long, rude noise.

They were standing together on a rutted road that led around the main building to the hotel entrance. On the left was a parking field. On the right, halfway to the hotel, were the living quarters of those who worked there. From out of this building, at the call of the whistle, came three men on the run, two of them wearing undershirts.

"Use your brains, son," growled the foghorn voice before the help had arrived. "Back out. You're makin' a big mistake." Then loudly for the others, he said: "A crasher." And now four of them stood holding the line.

"O.K., fella," one of them declared, "O.K."

"Hold it right there, son," said another.

"Just back out, fella, and everything will be all right," said a third.

Four men faced him now, and yet Val could think of nothing better at the moment than a good fight. It never settled anything, he knew, but then again neither did anything else. There before him stood the animated stupidity of the whole world. His only wish was to smash open the entire evening as though it were just so much glass.

He took one step back; they all took one step forward. He tried it again and again it happened. It was like some insane vaudeville

act, and Val decided to end it by scattering them over the countryside like a bunch of stuffed dummies. His fury was like a great pack
on his back. Then came realization. *None of this was new!* They had
faced this problem many times before. He could tell by the way they
were handling him. *He was not unique!* With a turn, Val paraded out
through the gate.

He marched along the blacked-out road thrusting his arm into
the open windows of parked cars. Finally, he found an Oldsmobile
with the keys still in place. Bright headlights cut through a wild
growth of grass and weeds to the base of the wall. In a moment they
were leading the way beneath lurking trees to where the doubled
guards were standing. One placed himself in Val's path, holding his
hand high, while the other strolled up to the car.

"I want to check in," Val said.

A face stared suspiciously into the window. Val was certain he
was recognized. He was wrong.

"O.K., pull up over there," ordered the guard, pointing to a row
of autos lined up at the hotel entrance. "I'll phone for a porter to
get your luggage."

Yelling came from behind him as he took instead a fork in the
road that led away from the hotel and brought him at top speed to
the parking field near the back gate where he and the four apes
had had their little dance. Now there was only one of them again
standing small and distant in the rear entrance beneath a pale
saucer of lamplight. Val kept driving, slowly down over bumps and
puddles, until he had circled around behind the hotel below which
was a serene, almost artificial reflection of lake. Abandoning the
Oldsmobile beside a pickup truck with THE GUARDIAN printed on its
side, he ran in the dark past trash cans stinking of wet rubbish and
spurted up a long flight of concrete steps tripping once in his blind-
ness. When he reached the top and faced a large swimming pool,
luminously green with underwater lights, he saw people dancing
near the diving board and only then felt pain from the fall on the
stairs. Music came from a juke box that had been moved to the doorway of the game room. No one was in the pool. Val moved across

a vast stretch of lawn where well-dressed couples stood in clusters, chatting. He passed among them with the secret satisfaction of a spy.

None of the guards were in the lobby, and quite a few females moved in the crowd. A lovely blank-faced girl in a gold lamé dress drifted stiffly across the carpet as though the least unnecessary movement would unravel her beauty. A long-haired *femme fatale* with her figure very much on display sat on the arm of a couch, looking at everyone but the man with whom she was speaking. Val chuckled at the tinseled opulence surrounding him and at all the blue suits and the white-on-white shirts and ties.

After searching the room twice, he went up to the desk and had her paged, and soon a bellboy passed through the lobby getting a few laughs with the name. Smoking a cigarette in one of the deep chairs where he could keep an eye out for guards coming in the front entrance, Val waited and hummed again the melody from Prokofiev. When she didn't appear, he went to the desk and asked that they connect him to her room.

"Be be be," parroted a precise desk clerk as he moved his finger down a list of names. "I'm sorry, sir, we have no one by that name at the hotel."

"Aren't all personnel from the MGM film staying here?"

"Yes, sir," said the mechanical clerk.

"Well, she's *one* of them."

"I'm sorry, sir, we have no one by that name at the hotel."

The mechanical eyes were hunting for someone better to serve. Was there a note for Val De Franco? The clerk turned his red back and thrust his hand into one of the mail slots. There he found an official blue card of some kind, read it, walked back to the desk, reached beneath it, and placed on the counter a white shoebox tied with a purple ribbon. Val guessed what it was as he carried it to a nearby couch, for one end was as heavy as stone. Setting eyes on it gave him a jolt, nevertheless. A Rolleiflex 2.8E with a built-in exposure meter and a leather case and strap. Better even than the one stolen. "Christ," he said, as he tore open the envelope, "how does she know I won't run *off* with the goddamn thing."

The note inside had been folded, opened, and refolded in several ways.

Hi:

I've had something of a battle with myself as to whether or not I should stand you up this way. The battle has proved itself negative due to no fault of my own (which I'm sure you would understand) and thus gave birth to my correspondence. Hence, I'm sorry.

You see, something has come up all of a sudden and by the time you read this missive I will be on my way back to New York through no fault of my own. I shall look you up in the city in a couple of weeks. That is, if it's O.K. with you. I'm sorry.

Your friend,
Honey Bea

P.S. By the bye, the camera is yours. Have fun.

There was a skunk on Lexington Avenue, and no one seemed to care. It waddled along, unlikely and curious, ticking the pavement with fleeting paws until it was pulled to a stop near the corner. At the upper end of its leash was an ex-hockey player in a green beret who stood in a stiff and proud pose at the intersection. A passing window washer, with pail and ladder, glanced at the animal with cold curiosity.

Val instructed the man with the leash to walk on while a woman, coming in the other direction, smiled at the animal with that condescending love most members of her sex extend to almost all things that move and are under three feet high. Noticing Val as he knelt on the pavement, the woman took care to keep out of camera range, unaware that a benignly smiling and horsey image of herself had already been captured on the emulsion. Another woman going giggely giggely goo as she leaned over a baby carriage, straightened with a back pain, saw the odd animal, and opened her mouth in amazement.

"That's a skunk."

"Deodorized, madam," scored the hockey player.

"Are you sure?"

"We're about 70 percent sure," Val said in mock helpfulness, and as the woman, still open-mouthed, pondered the seven to three odds and their margin of safety she, too, was captured for all time with a faint, precise shutter snap.

"Nice to know that people can still be shaken up," Val remarked afterward, as they entered the brownstone where the owner lived with his pet. "When people lose their pomposity, will this world be an *ever* dull place."

In the one-room flat, Val shouldered the strobe he had borrowed from Ulysses (his own was on the blink again) and with bounce light he finished up with a few final shots. After a brief chat and the obtaining of a release, he descended the brownstone steps two at a time, shaking his head in smiling amazement. A few blocks away he stopped and snapped his fingers. "The name," said Val to three girls holding three large ice cream cones. "I forgot to ask what he named the goddamn thing." Into a drugstore phone booth he went for a quick call to the room he had just left. He rattled the door open a minute later and spoke aloud to an old man buying razor blades. "Malcolm, for crysake!" And with strobe box and camera dangling, he continued his march downtown.

It was nearing five o'clock, and Manhattan's daily exodus was beginning. Though almost every conceivable human type was now to be seen in the busy streets, Val's consciousness was in tune with the cadence of high heels. He made his way through the crowds, moving from one woman to another as would a swimmer from one island to another, keeping close but not stopping. "Ah, you Bronx temptress," he mumbled to himself. Of another he said: "Yes, dear, that *is* quite a dress. How the boys in the office must love it." And then loud enough for a third young lady to hear: "What *have* you done to your tresses? Oh, you *wild* creature."

He entered the shabbiest door on the street, one with no address on it at all, and slowly climbed the metal-tipped stairs to the tilt-floored anteroom where Ulysses, in a buttoned-down paisley sport shirt, sat absorbed in the inspection of contract prints. As Val walked downhill on the linoleum floor, he recognized with a jolt that a new photograph had been mounted on the wall. There she was in sharp color half seated on a high stool with one hand cupping her jet-black hair, the other resting crudely on her hip, and a long memorable leg extended to the floor in classic display. She was dressed in that glamour cliché of costumes: bra, brief panties, and meshed stockings, one of which was rolled down just enough to flash the sight of clean-legged skin. In an effort to improve on her anatomy, she had sucked in her stomach, thrown back her shoulders, and breathed out her none-too-prominent breasts. The open-toed, high-heeled shoes and the round glistening earrings, Val recognized as her own. But that look transformed her into something utterly arrogant and almost totally unfamiliar, an impostor under glass encouraging covetous looks from inside the flat, impenetrable world of Ektachrome.

"When did you do this, for crysake?" he asked, angrily.

"Months ago, keed," said the gray-haired Negro. "But you could tell it was my work, huh?"

"She looks like Tony Canzoneri."

"Who's he?"

"He was a boxer, you clown."

"Well, I could tell you didn't like it."

"I love it," said Val, placing the strobe on the desk and falling into a wooden chair. "Where'd you get that shirt?"

"Macy's."

"Got to get me a few like it."

"How'd it go today?"

Val was staring at the photo across the room. "How did what go today?"

"With the skunk."

From behind the drawn curtain came men's voices.

"You got a good crowd tonight?" Val asked, hanging an arm over the back of the chair.

"Fourteen."

"Well, well." He pulled at his tie although the knot had already been loosened and the collar opened. "Pretty good."

From inside came a woman's rough laughter.

"That Utah? God what a voice."

Ulysses tilted back on the hind legs of his chair, parted the curtain slightly from the doorjamb, and checked the goings on in the next room. His chair bucked, landing back on all fours, and Val was caught looking at Tanya again.

"She was in here two days ago," Ulysses said, "working."

"Uh, huh."

Someone was descending heavily from the law office above them, making his way on down the stairs into the street.

"She asked about you."

"Uh, huh."

"Tell me, keed, how come you two never got back together? Or am I gettin' too personal?" He laughed diplomatically.

"You want to know? You *really* want to know?"

"Well, the reason I asked, keed, is 'cause you two kinda went well together."

"Her analyst has a whole theory on me. He said I'm afraid of commitment on all levels. A unique case, he said, because I hardly own anything. I move from city to city, apartment to apartment, job to job, girl to girl. Nothing worries me, nothing concerns me, nothing holds me. The perfectly self-sufficient man. Well, Tan tried to get me to go to him so he could change this. I went once just for kicks. Cost me twenty bills, but it was worth it. Never had such a ball. I made up an absurd answer to every question. I said my father was weak and saintly and that my old lady was a shit. You know how I met Tan? In this queer party in the Village. So I told him I was gay. 'But you sleep with Miss Lando rather successfully,' he said. 'Yes,' I said, 'but when I sleep with her, I imagine I'm sleeping with movie stars. When I'm with her,' I said, 'I imagine I'm with oh say Tab Hunter or Rock Hudson or somebody.' Should have seen his face. It was *worth* twenty bucks."

"The question, keed, was why didn't you go back?"

"'Cause I didn't like the guy. He looked queer to me, actually."

"No, I mean go back to her. You and Tanya."

"Oh, that. Hey, you Black Moslem, don't you ever have any liquor in this joint?"

"Not a drop. Sorry."

"You're a goddamn sadist, you know that?"

"Come on, keed, answer the question."

"I tried, you bastard. I tried to get together. I called her a couple of times, but she either wasn't home or she wouldn't answer."

"And after that?"

"Hell, I don't know. After that I got involved with this other broad." Val breathed a secluded laugh, and then pronounced her name with theatrical thoroughness: "Francheska Luca."

"She the one who likes to be beaten?"

"The very same."

"And what about Tanya?"

"The bitch walked out. So let her stay out or walk back in again. What the hell."

Ulysses leaned back to check inside the studio, then sat forward again. "I just don't understand you two."

"Neither do we."

"Well, look out, man," said the Negro with a smile. "She said she just might marry me one of these days."

"Do tell?"

"Said she would on one condition."

"Oh?"

"That I'd agree to bring up our children white."

"She always was a million laughs, that girl."

"So you're free of her and no regrets?"

"Free with no regrets."

"The next question, I guess, is why do you look so miserable?"

"It's this damn business. I'm not a free-lance photographer. I'm a free-lance slave. Moneymoneymoney. Grub for it day and night. Each new job is like starting from scratch. The bastard who invented money fixed us but good."

"What you need, keed, is a stable income. Something that will leave you free for other things. For better things."

"Let's just say other things."

"Well, how about it?"

"How about what, for crysake?"

"Taking over this place for me."

"You are mad."

"Three thousand, I'm asking, keed. Just three grand."

"And I'm to go three grand into debt for what?"

While more laughter came from inside, Ulysses kept his chocolate face turned toward Val whose own features seemed to recede in time until he became once again a despondent little boy.

"This place can make bread for you, keed. The rest of the time you can be out doing the work you should have been doing the last two years."

"You sound like a grade B movie, for crysakes. The wife says, darling, you must go back and complete your concerto. Sometimes she says your sonata. Have you noticed it's never a violin partita or a quintet for flute and strings."

"But what about my offer? Come on, man, I want to sell out and move south."

"You know somethin'? You're absolutely the only Negro in the country who wants to move south."

"My daughter lives in Birmin'ham."

"Then bring her up here, fast."

"Can't, keed, she lives with her husband and children. I want to go down there to spend my declinin' years."

"Bastard, you're using pathos on me. Out-and-out pathos."

"I'm serious. I want you to grab this place. I could sell it for twice more than I'm asking you to pay. Listen, man, commit yourself." Cracking a smile. "Think how happy Tanya's analyst will be."

Val was about to hit him with a pizza crust from an ashtray, when the curtain was shunted aside and out marched the men. Most of them made thunder on the stairs while the usual lingerers asked questions about coming schedules until finally they, too, disappeared, sending up faint noises from the street. Val leaned back in his chair watching the red fluorescent light appear and reappear around the edge of the drawn blinds and reflect across the glassed photographs on the wall.

"How's she been?" Val asked with a wounded look.

"She's fine. She's all hopped up about tryin' to win the lead role in some play or other."

"Summer stock?"

"That's not what she said. She said off-Broadway."

"Well, well."

"Yeh, she's doin' fine. Low on money as per usual. But O.K. Lookin' good. Kinda real excited about her chances in this play. She seemed happy."

"So she's surviving without me. No ex-lover wants to hear that."

"Maybe she's pinin' for you, keed."

"Pine for this scarecrow," said Utah. "Forget it."

Holding open the curtain and garbed in summer white, with matching eye patch and hatbox, was a hefty, haughty red-haired wench who stood before them in seductive array making the most of her dramatic-comic entrance.

"It's the fair Ophelia," said Val, not even bothering to look.

"Hey, Pops, is some poor chick actually dipsy over this rake? Tell her to take the knife. Tell her to forget it."

From inside his desk, bought nine years ago from the Salvation Army, Ulysses removed a green metal strongbox, unlocked it, and gave Utah ten dollars.

"Thanks, boss-man. When you want me again?"

"How 'bout," he checked his calendar, "next Thursday?"

"Okey-doke and I hope a different crew of goons shows up. One guy wanted me to stand on my head. Can you beat that. I told him, *forget* it. I said, boys, at *Minsky's* I'll do it, but here for you louts? Get lost."

"What did you think of the new girl?" the Negro asked in a whisper.

"Yeh, is she for real?"

"Do the men like her?"

"With me around, baby, it's kinda hard to tell."

"You know something?" Val broke in. "I've seen every part of you but your left eye."

"Yeh," said Utah, grinning at her own exit line. "Always keep something hidden." She halted and faced them from the doorway. "When you going to pop over for some junk, playboy?"

"Anon, anon," said Val, waving her away.

"And I mean *junk*," she stressed. To Ulysses: "This one. He comes up, drinks my liquor, eats my food, wipes his dirty feet on my rug, makes a pass, and then what does he buy? Nothing. A bag of pot every month or two. Big deal. Forget it."

"If we're revealing secrets, you bitch, I'll tell about the time you got a Coke bottle caught in your ... "

"That's libelous, you mother-fucker."

"Shhhh." Ulysses indicated the new model still inside dressing.

"Bye-bye, Daddy-o. And listen, playboy, why don't you come up and see my left eye sometime?"

Val listened to her heels do violence to the stairs. "She's a swamp, that one. But a great kid. Someday she'll get booked on everything from indecent exposure to narcotics addiction. She'll get forty years in the electric chair, and I for one will be sad to see her go."

Ulysses had removed the money from the strongbox and was counting it with mute lips and quick fingers. The sight of wealth suspended Val in mid-thought.

"You made all *that* today?"

"Today and yesterday."

"I'm impressed."

"You should stay away from that one," said Ulysses, nodding his gray head toward the street.

"Why? I haven't made her yet."

"You don't want to be in her pad when the shamuses close in."

"The hell I don't. That's one of my great regrets. Do you real-ize that I've never been arrested. Never. Not for causing a brawl or impersonating a queer or smoking pot or statutory rape or for speeding even. Think of the experience I've missed. And you tell me not to hang around Utah. Do you realize that she's been jailed three times already and she's just twenty-four? I *want* to get arrested."

"You drive yourself too hard."

"I'm not joshing, kid-o."

"What'll it win you, this getting jailed?"

"I can't explain it. New experiences thrill me."

"Or is it just to be able to say, I've been arrested. Hot damn."

"That's part of it. Like I can say I once played Cassius in Chicago. Like I can say that the Modern Museum of Art has one of my oils in their lending library. Or that I once made Miss Rheingold and Miss America in the same week. Or that I once turned five dollars into five hundred dollars at Vegas in one night. Or that I drank..."

"O.K., I'm impressed."

"You're impressed? You're shocked and you know it."

"Shocked? At the life you lead? No, keed, I'm too old to be shocked. I'm too smart to be envious. What's left? I'm impressed."

"Balls," said Val, getting to his feet for no reason and having nothing to do with himself once he got there. The money was being replaced in the strongbox. "What did you take in? What did it come to?"

"It came to enough to make you right happy if you owned this place."

"There you go again." He circled the room while Ulysses locked the desk and fastened the key to his inside pocket with a safety pin. "Own this place. That's all I need."

Pops slipped several sheets of contact prints beneath a blotter and gathered up an array of paper clips. "Well, I'm not waitin' forever. I'm goin' to sell this place to somebody, if not you. I'm finished."

The downhill linoleum floor seemed to urge Val toward the wall and the picture where Tanya sat on the stool posturing a grotesque charade of desire. Across the photograph, the image of Ulysses rose tall and straight as his body rose from behind the desk going off to perform the last few chores before closing up. Tanya was alone again behind glass: alone for a moment only, for in the reflected doorway the curtain was fumbled with and finally lifted instead of pulled aside, and out into the reflection of the room she stepped, her face superimposed upon Tanya's, her mouth opening in calm surprise: "Well, Val De Franco, as I live and breathe."

The taxi leaped forward, missed the light, breached it anyway, and swung down Sixth Avenue at top speed, avoided a near broadside with another car and screeched to a halt at the next light.

"He drives like a Keystone Cop," she said, readjusting her hair once the flood of wind had stopped. A delayed-reaction laugh at her own remark was innocent with surprise.

"Incredible meeting you this way," said Val. "We'll celebrate something fierce." His heels were bouncing as he sat. "I feel elated. I feel like flying."

"You look it, you really do."

The taxi leaped forward, rolling their heads in unison.

"Where are you heading?" she asked, curious as to their destination.

"For a while there I thought it was into business. Now it's to the nearest bar. A far wiser choice. Hereherehere. Whoa, driver. Land here."

He bounced out. She slid, ducked, and rose up after him. The city skipped a beat and all was quiet. Val inhaled the warm, benevolent evening and grinned at the sight of her: all in black, even down to her stockings and shoes. The glamour getup of her first appearance and the peasant earthiness of her second had given way to the Village beat, the sexy little sideshow with a sly, charming, and slightly fraudulent smile.

Twin drinks stood before them on the bar. The arid stillness of the cocktail lounge was suspended in an atmosphere of back lighting and clinical readiness.

Honey Bea was saying: "And I only worked there as a waitress for three whole days. But I'm quitting because the owner won't let me be. He says he's got this real thing for me, and I believe I know what thing he's referring to." She continued working loose the last match from a cardboard pack while a filter-tip Parliament was already poised and wobbling between her lips. "So he said to me that good girls sleep around as much these days as bad ones."

Val watched the tip of her cigarette glow red in the flame.

"So I said, that's entirely likely, Mr. Random. That's entirely…"

"Before I forget," he interrupted her, no longer able to hold back the flood of questions, "I owe you twenty dollars and I haven't forgotten. Just want you to know. Now whose camera *is* this?" He placed the Rollei on the bar. "And how did you get hold of it?"

"The camera, is it a good one?"

"The best. Now how in hell did you get it?"

"From a photographer at the hotel."

"He gave it to you?"

"Him? Fat chance."

"Don't tell me you bought it, for crysake?"

She leaned back on the stool, and the black cotton mounds demonstrating her breasts moved in a tremor of mirth.

"Well, we're back to the same question again. How did you get…" About to sip from his whiskey sour, he returned it to the bar top. "Wait a minute, don't tell me *that's* the way you got it?"

Honey clamped her upper teeth on her lower lip and pretended contrition while a man who bore a striking resemblance to Dean Acheson entered the room and ordered a drink.

"Just to get me a camera you went ahead and…For *me*, who you didn't even…? Oh, come on, not really?"

"Remember it was as much for me as it was for you. I didn't know I was going to have to leave town the next day, I really didn't." She looked at him over the rim of her drink and swallowed.

"But still and all…"

"Why not? He deserved it, I can tell you."

"*Deserved?* I don't get it. You gave yourself to him and then you say…"

"Gave? *Gave?*" This time there was nothing remote about her laughter. She even lost her balance on the stool, screamed, and gripped the bar ledge with pouncing hands. Several people looked up, then down again into their drinks with expressions melting back into melancholy. The man who had just entered the bar continued staring after the others had turned away and watched her give Val a frisky shot in the arm.

"That's not the way I got the camera." Her voice threatened another toboggan of laughter. "I *stole* it."

"You *stole* it?" Val was delighted. "Little wide-eyed and innocent you? But why from him? Who the hell is he anyway?"

"Oh, once he played a dirty trick on me, that's all."

"What kind of trick?"

She took aim at him across the rim of her drink. "I'm going to get all angry again if I start talking about it. And when I get angry, I get angry."

"Is that a fact?"

"Yup, that is right, sir."

"Well, I have nothing against owning stolen goods. Why, come to think of it..."

"Oh, I'm so glad you're not one of those all hot in the pants with moral fervor. Why, if you know what that man did to me you'd send me back to steal more."

"Hell, I have half a mind to send you back anyway. Between you and me I could use a telephoto lens. No, I'm not one of those all hot in the pants with moral fervor."

"It's a good thing."

"But I'd love to hear why you hate him so."

"Maybe someday I'll tell you."

"I'll try to be patient."

"You do that little thing." She cupped her little chin and giggled.

"Barkeep!" He held up the victory sign.

"Don't you think the bartender looks like Paul Douglas? He does, doesn't he? I mean it. Stop laughing. He does, doesn't he? Did you see *Letter to Three Wives?* That Jeanne Crain looks so young for a mother of five. I really..."

"Talking of movies..."

"And you know who you look like? You look like a Jack Palance who's seen too many Roddy McDowall movies."

Val leaned closer to her, his nose all but touching hers. "You won't believe this, you just won't. But you're the first person who *ever* said that to me."

"Oh, I believe you," she replied seriously. "I'm very proceptive that way."

"*Proceptive?*"

"Yes, I can just look at someone and then tell them what movie actor they look like, and people usually agree. Other people, that is."

"Who do *you* look like?" he asked.

"Gloria Grahame and Carroll Baker. Sort of a cross between them." She nodded in self-agreement. "Except I sort of got bigger boobies." She pressed four fingers over her mouth at her own audaciousness.

Val tousled her hair. "Now listen to me, woman. I was talking about movies. When I met you, you were doing a bit part in one. And you're obviously still modeling. So how come this waitress business, if I may ask?"

"You keep buying me drinks, love, and you can ask me anything your little heart desires." And she gave him a sly look of dubious meaning.

"Except what that photographer did to you?"

"That's correct, sir."

"MGM hasn't sent me my check yet," she continued, gazing into the depth of her new drink. "And the money from modeling," snapping her fingers, "like that it goes. But I have another job tomorrow afternoon. So for a while it's all right."

"A job. Who with? What photographer?"

"Him," she said, her index finger curving against the joint as she pointed to the Rollei on the bar.

Val, lifting his drink, put it down again. "Good grief, from the joker you *stole* this from?"

"Shhhh. Why not? He bought himself another one. It's not like he hasn't got a camera."

There was a muffled explosion at her feet, a jarring clatter that disrupted the pious tableau of the cocktail lounge.

"That's for me," said Honey, sliding off the stool and reaching into her bag. She ended the calamity and then brandished an antique alarm clock. "It's the reminder. Got to make a call."

Her spiked heels hammered like the strokes of a gavel. Chins lifted, eyes became industrious, and the cocktail shaker in the bartender's hands slightly lost acceleration.

Left with an alarm clock in one hand and a drink in the other, Val arranged them in a still life along with the camera and the pretzel bowl. He listened to the hollow striding ka-tick-ka-tock coming from the fat, vapid face of the timepiece. And he watched the stoic bartender slap down a cardboard coaster and raise his eyebrows questioningly to a new customer. Sitting at the bar, he had been content with her. Now that she had gone for a few moments, he discovered that he hadn't been content at all. He had simply been vacant while she had entertained, puzzled, and occupied him. She was bedworthy, stupid, at times delightful, certainly friendly, and he could tell that she gave a twitch to almost every man in the room. Still, she wasn't Tanya. She wasn't anything like Tanya (which would have been worse), and therefore he found her unique but inadequate. He didn't want her, so he decided to seduce the girl and be done with it.

Chins lifted at the sound of her approach. Her features (three parts Gloria Grahame to one part Carroll Baker) were stilled with sadness. It could have been anything from a death in the family to a run in the stocking. Hers was not a face agile with expression. Dark immobile eyebrows, straw-blond hair, a playful nose, that pert chin, the lips implying passion but perhaps for nothing more than a popsicle. All these features, joined without finesse, added up to a face that was not to be taken quite seriously, and a face that gave no warning of the body below.

"You get your call through?"

Her assorted features became smudged with disgust, and ending her attempts to mount the stool, she spoke in secrecy out of the corner of her mouth.

"Let's get out of here."

"Why? What's the ...?" He followed the slight tilt of her head and noticed a police officer who had strolled in to chat with the owner.

"It's just a ... "

"I hate cops," she declared, snatching her alarm clock from the bar. "Let's cut out."

In the taxi she oppressed him with her nonstop chatter, although one of her mannerisms he found romantically promising. To make her point, to regain his attention, to encourage him to share her laughter she would touch his knee, or prod his arm or press his wrist or scold him with a shove at the shoulder. A touch-talker. He liked this. Yet for the rest, she hid herself in pointless conversation, disappearing like a squid into a cloud of her own ink.

As she clattered up the four flights, he strode the stairs behind her two at a time. When asked again why she hated the police, she jolted her shoulders in an abrupt shrug and kept climbing. "Oh, what a cute apartment," she exclaimed. "I really mean it." He kicked a pair of underpants up, over, and behind the bed, and then gave her a guided tour through the cluttered room. "This is the living room," he said of the couch. "And this," pointing to the radio, "is the music room." The photo enlarger was the darkroom. Two shelves of books were the library. The sink was called the kitchen and the brass bed comprised the guest and master bedroom. She grazed him with a smile. Then she noticed what he had hung on the walls. "Oh, pictures, goodie. Oh, they're wonderful, they really are." He sprang upon the bed, and using his umbrella as a pointer, offered a brief gallery lecture while Honey sat down on the dust-ejecting couch and listened with an overly diligent look of attention. "And what about that one?" she asked, twisting about and selecting an 8 × 10 behind her. "Her name is Francheska Luca," Val explained. "A flaming redhead. A one-time model for Miss Clairol ads, and a supreme pain in the ass. This one was taken in the studio. Her nipples were coated with lipstick, which is why they look so red." "She good in bed?" Honey smiled playfully. "Well," said Val, jumping up and down on the mattress, "who isn't these days?"

"And what's with her?" she asked as Val climbed down to pick up his drink. "You left her out." She was pointing with a middle finger at a swarthy beauty above the dresser.

He bit his fingernail and studied the photo anew.

"She's great-lookin'," Honey conceded.

Val removed the hangnail from his lips, sipped his Jack Daniels, then returned it to his teeth. "That was taken a year ago .... Available light with a mirror reflector .... Pan X ... f/3.5 at a 50th."

"Boy did you ever get technical all of a sudden. I asked about *her*."

"All right, we'll talk about her. Let me see. She's one of those perceptive people who has something nice to say against everyone. She's a bitch with a lovely life pattern. She keeps falling in love with the wrong men and then crucifies them for not being the right ones. She has all the misguided fury of the newly born liberal. She's hip, witty, and intelligent and one of those obsessive show-biz types who hunts fame like a female Ahab. She can sing, dance and act, and what she doesn't know about life you could put into a book, adapt it to the stage and sell it to Hollywood. She's flirtatious, argumentative and middle-class. And she's wasting her life away because nine years ago the holy voices told her to go forth and save the American stage. Who'll save her? I have no idea. She stands for everything that attracts me in women, which explains why I am hopelessly doomed. Because she's not a woman at all. She's a clever, personable glamour machine. She's a success engine in high gear. She's the glove of steel upon the velvet hand. Her name? Emma Kretchmar. To hell with her. Here's to you, H.B. Wait, have some more. Comeoncomeoncomeoncomeon. You want another ice cube?

O.K., here's to you. My female Mount Everest with breasts. Lavisher of cameras. Lender of monies. Giver of small delights. A living rebate on a teenage fantasy. A microcosm of the ..."

"A female Mount Everest with breasts? *Wha?*"

"A symbolic reference, my dear. A mythical concept. Like the Bible, not to be taken literally."

"Oh ... I think I understand."

"She thinks she understands. Swell."

Giving up all hope, Val folded himself into a chair. Her seeming vacuousness enveloped the room with a chill that numbed him. No, he would *not* take her to bed and be done with it. This time he decided to make a conscious effort to avoid that, to back off from grappling with her chunky body. He only hoped the job of getting rid of her would not take long.

"It's getting late," she observed to his immense delight.

"Yes, it's getting very late. Yes, it is."

A neighbor's spaniel barked eight times; then four more times; then stopped. A courtyard dachshund squeaked in harsh reply. Honey began a monologue, relating the entire plot of the latest John Wayne epic by way of making a point which in the end eluded her.

Val was vacant, filling up with daydreams and playthings. He had idle visions of smashing windows with long broom handles, of tossing furniture off high roofs. He even tried to will himself to Europe, but stubbornly his body remained where it was. He goosed Madam Nu, boxed Joe Louis, and resurrected his road company characterization of Cassius. Yet he ended up back in the same damn broken-springed armchair, shaking his drink to hear the ice and not her chatter which all at once he realized had now amazingly ceased. In fact, she had vanished from the couch altogether. Only her drink remained, wedged upright between two cushions. In this same room Tanya had run out on him, and despite himself, he tossed a hard, anxious look at the door. It was closed as it should be, and his jacket, like a deflated image of himself, hung from the knob.

She was seated on the bed pulling off her turtle-neck sweater, her hair standing briefly on end like a sudden yellow flame. Her bra, too, was black. Collapsing a black cotton stocking, she revealed her enamel thigh, a nubbled knee, a slack calf. Then the stocking was tossed with the sweater over the brass bar of the bed where it hung like a snakeskin.

Val sat forward with plastered astonishment while the other stocking was slipped off with unctuous grace. He was thrilled by the chance discovery of a vast moral void. Rhythms of vitality were once again his, and he suddenly cherished this girl as he would a rare gift. Well, I've finally found her, he thought, someone even more promiscuous than me. Off came her skirt as well, and she had not so much as glanced at him. Without a work spoken, he lit a candle near the bed and turned off the lights. Removing his shirt and pants, letting them drop as he moved, he wedged his way into the narrow space between bed and wall to wrestle the window closed. When he stretched out on the mattress and looked around, Honey was missing again. His eyes shot to the door, to her clothes. He waited. Her head appeared from where she had knelt to arrange her shoes beneath the bed. Then, still kneeling, she placed both hands on the mattress, clasped them tightly and bowed her head. That evening, there seemed to be no end to his astonishment. As he stared at her in dumb amusement, she at last stood up, hunched briefly, and released her bra. To remove her panties, she dipped downward as though touching her toes in exercise. Finally she lay beside him, the candlelight quivering on the mountain range of her yellow skin.

"Wild! Do you *always* pray before making love?"

"I pray before going to sleep."

"That's the way children pray, kneeling."

"Yes, I think it's kind of cute, don't you?"

"But sweetie-pie, you're not a child anymore."

"In some ways, we are always children, we really are."

"Are you very religious?"

"Oh, no. I'm not religious at all."

"Then why the prayer bit?"

"I think it's kind of nice. Really. Going to church and all. And the music. Everybody should go. It's pleasant, don't you think?"

"To whom do you pray?"

"To God."

"Tsh, then you *are* religious."

"How can I be, silly, when I don't believe in him?"

"Then why the hell do you pray to him, you nut?"

"Well, I don't believe in Santa Claus either, yet I ... "

"*What?* You mean to tell me you don't believe in Santa? You *are* a wicked girl."

"Oh, you're teasing me, aren't you? I pray because ... well, it keeps me from gettin' lonely."

"What exactly do you pray about? Clue me in."

"I pray for all nice things. Like I pray for Eddie Fisher. That he'll find himself a new wife and all. I pray for jobs for me and weekends at the beach. I just love the beach, I really do. Do you want to know what I prayed for just now?"

"Yes, go ahead, what?"

"I prayed just now for us. That we'll be good and all."

"Good? You mean virtuous?"

"No, silly. Good. Good *together.*"

"You mean good in *bed?*"

"That's important, don't you think?"

"Holey moley." Val fell back into the pillow. "A goddamn amoral saint, that's what she is."

"I just love your laugh, you know that? I do. You have so much energy. I wonder where you get it all."

He sat up, finished his drink and, still snickering, placed the glass on the windowsill. Honey was wringing her ear, her glass already empty and out of sight.

"Well, shall we begin?" she asked, pleasantly.

"Why not?"

"What the hell, huh?" She was teasing his lack of enthusiasm.

"Might as well," he said, teasing her back, "before the prayer gets cold."

"Oh, you're terrible, you really are."

Wherever he touched her body, her supple flesh yielded like a soft rug, and almost at once a series of deep, gentle gasps intensified her look of distress. Without warning, she clutched and wrestled his skeletal frame like an avenging warrior, and together they rolled backward through the ages into belching primeval mud.

There was an interval of rest. Val lay back as she recharged their drinks which they only partly consumed before she began her second assault. This time he paid more attention (his senses floundering less), and as he in turn crouched upon and then under and then behind and then upon her again, he got the impression that she was wriggling in a solitary tempest, that he could have changed places with another man and left the room and she wouldn't have known the difference. How do you conquer a woman who at the very moment of submission doesn't even recognize your presence?

He sank into a dark fatigue, and the light barely reached him. The past few nights of insomnia pressed down, and he squinted the candle flame into long sharp streaks until the bed was cleaved in half by some soundless cosmic axe so that he and she were drifting separately on twin couches in a warm fluid room.

A voice nuzzled his distracted mind, and he was awake without warning.

"Are you sure? What did you say? You'll have to speak louder than..." Honey squatting naked by the couch held the phone to her ear with both hands. "How is..." What'd you say? She wants me? Oh, I wish she'd leave me alone for once. All right, hold your water. I said, all right. I'll be there soon...In twenty minutes...Yes, bye."

Still crouching, she said: "Oh, you're awake. I'm sorry, I didn't mean..."

"Where are you going?"

"Don't you worry. You just go back to sleep."

"I'm not worrying. I'm curious."

She pulled on her skirt and sweater as he watched.

"Is someone sick?"

"Yes." Her stockings and underclothes she dumped in her bag.

"Who?"

"Don't worry yourself. I'm sorry I woke you." She kicked back her leg and put on her shoe. Changing hands on the dresser, she put on her other one.

"Who's sick, for crysake?"

About to flee, she came to the bed, armed with her clothes, and gave him a brief, dehydrated kiss.

"Who's sick? You going to tell me or not?"

Standing straight, holding her bag. "My aunt."

"What's wrong with her?"

"Cancer. Shall I blow out the candle or what? Oh, don't get up."

"Where will I get in touch with you?" he asked, following her synchronized rump across the room.

"Listen, love, let me call you." She opened the door. "I don't have a phone."

"Well, where the hell do you live?"

"Don't worry, silly." A moist soul kiss in the candlelight. Cotton and wool against his naked skin. "I'll call you. I really will."

"But what…"

Her lips again, a final, feeble good-by kiss, all sound and no pressure. "Got to run, love." And so she did, starting down the smelly stairs in the decrepit light of the ceiling bulb, clenching and unclenching her palm in farewell.

But she didn't call. A week later he began inquiries. Ulysses had neither her address nor telephone. It seemed that when she wanted work she called him; otherwise he never heard from her. Val dropped around two days later and still there was no news. A phone call the next day got the same results. Out of sheer perversity he decided to cease asking. He knew it was hardly progress to free himself from the loss of one woman only to replace it with the loss of another.

And he conjured up another problem as well. Of late, the constant repetition of quick, cheap magazine stories, the deadening repertoire of cheesecake postures imposed on vain, sluggish girls, the mundane photos of "junked up" nightclub singers frowning face-forward in the blues, the pert pony-tailed dancers exercising their obsession in bleak rehearsal halls, the conceited actors performing the role of the modest husband at home, of late all this and the rest of it left him in arid boredom.

He failed to set up jobs in advance because he was too uninterested to bother. The money still came in, though less and less, and the jobs he did manage to complete and sell seemed to enervate his spirit. Now the entreaties of Ulysses Hill grew frighteningly seductive. A studio with a wealth of steady customers willing to pay every night to take pictures of beautiful women or to go with him on a Sunday field trip upstate, a studio to rent out mornings and afternoons to free-lance cameramen who needed a professional setup to do a job, a studio with a beach ball, a beach chair, a beach umbrella, a white plastic pedestal, a flat wooden bench, a bus stop sign, three stools of different heights, fish netting, and a black contour chair, a studio with three floodlights, each on a tripod stand and two clamp lights (one that usually hung from the ceiling and one that almost never worked), a studio with several backdrops that rolled down from the ceiling like giant hand towels, one yellow, one green, and one blue—all his for three thousand dollars to be paid back over four years. Did he want it? He still didn't think he did.

During this general drift of his disinterest with playful images of Honey Bea out of range in the daylight and a constant sense of Tanya unreachable in the dark, Val dropped up to Utah's apartment on Thompson Street one midafternoon to persuade her to sleep with him. It took, all told, thirty-five minutes.

"Well, well, here he is," said the voluptuous cyclops as she opened the door. "The one-man rat pack."

Val stepped carefully across the rug which was strewn with photographs to be inserted in her album.

"Just curious to see if the police had caught you yet."

"Arrest me?" She struck a pose that was irrelevant but effective. "Forget it."

When she saw that he had no intention of buying any of her "junk" and that he was obviously bent on swift seduction, she became peeved. Folding her hands around one of her knees and rocking back and forth on the couch, she peered at him with her visible eye (the patch on the other was red to match her shoes) and asked: "What have you got in mind, Daddy-o?"

He poured two bourbons, sat beside her and had her sew a button on his jacket. Then in dulcet tones, he told her that she was a lovely, vivacious, castrating beauty, and he stroked her red hair and slipped his hand under her dress. She snapped at him angrily: "What do you think—I fuck just like that? I have to be in love first."

"How many dates does it take you to fall in love?" he asked with a sarcasm that was completely missed.

"Hard to say," she answered, thoughtfully, "maybe six, maybe seven."

"Well, we've known each other for quite a while now. Isn't that worth something? A few dates at least?"

"Well, maybe a few. Hey, you trying to con me or something?"

"How can you think of such a thing?" he said, as two dozen Utahs eyed him from the floor. Hadn't he bought pot from her continually for six whole months and hadn't he sent up junkies now and then for a quick fix? Why, they were soul mates is what they were. But she wasn't convinced. They discussed it over another round of drinks. Presently the mood in the room changed while three Venetian slats fluttered in chronic cross-ventilation. Val's stealthy palm persisted on her solid thigh as he guided his breath, soft and sibilant, into her tepid ear.

Thirty-five minutes in all. Then she said: "You're in luck, Daddy-o."

"How so?"

"It's my twenty-seventh day. It comes tomorrow."

"Oh?"

"I hate to let my twenty-seventh day go to waste."

He began unbuttoning her dress at once. But first a shower and off she went while Val strolled around her furnished room, listening to the muffled waterfall. Tacked up on the wall was a news photo of Miss Utah De Lux in a polkadot two-piece bathing suit with matching eye patch. The attached story was headlined *The Girl in the Three-Piece Bikini*. Other shots stared at him from the four walls. As though this weren't enough, there she was grinning, pouting, sprawling, laughing and squatting all over the floor. The accumulative effect set him thinking, and he snapped his fingers. He was supposed to call Ulysses about something or other, and he sat down to dial the number he should have dialed two hours ago.

"I'm about to indulge in some hanky-panky," he said, chewing a piece of ice. "I wanted you to be the first to know."

"She's here, keed," said the soft voice.

"Who is?" He felt closed in, encumbered.

"Miss Bea just this minute walked in."

The note, vertical like a cardiogram and legible though rushed, said the following: With tumultuous ambivalence I find I am suddenly called away. The phone is indeed a wicked device. Faretheewell my one-eyed beauty. Remember me. In twenty-eight days I shall return.

In the elevator he had second thoughts. Ambivalence. Was it e-l-a-n-c-e or a-l-e-n-c-e? He couldn't recall. In the taxi he toyed with the idea of phoning in his corrections. This kept him smiling until he flew up the stairs and into the studio. Seated on the desk, fixing a broken sandal, and dressed in the same peasant outfit he had seen her wearing in the country, was the woman he wanted. Or was she? He asked her where she had been. Out of town, in Boston, was her answer. A modeling job. How was her aunt? Her aunt was fine. You mean she recovered from cancer? She didn't mean she had recovered from cancer. She meant that she was the same, as good as could be expected. She added that Val was looking very handsome. No, she wasn't trying to change the subject. He looked very handsome, he really did. She also wanted to know what he paid for that suit. "Twenty-four plus tax in Klein's." said Val. "Not in dollars, in kleins." Ulysses advised him to guard against her flattery. She could be a dangerous little girl, he claimed. "Is that right?" Val asked, "*are you dangerous?*" Honey laughed pleasantly and took Val out to buy her something to eat.

At the bar at McGinnis', while she chewed a hamburger, he listened as she talked about any number of nonsensical things, of movies and actors, of modeling and clothes, and he realized that he didn't want her after all, and so decided to take her once more and be done with it. She had gone off to make one of her mysterious phone calls, and when she returned he asked her a question which he was sure she would evade; but she didn't at all. A little hotel, she said, on Twenty-third Street. Why stay there of all places? he asked.

"It's a bird hotel," Honey said. "Cheap, cheap."

"Let's go there now."

"First a movie."

"Oh, you're kidding?"

"There's one on Forty-second Street. Rock Hudson and Doris Day and..."

"All right, if you'd rather see a movie instead of..."

It was the wrong question to ask. She wept helplessly during the first feature and laughed faithfully during the second, a transfixed, frightened, happy and most gullible little girl.

"Wasn't that sad the way they were wheeling Doris Day to the delivery room," said Honey as they emerged from the unfriendly chill of the air-conditioned theater, "with Rock Hudson running alongside getting married to her at the last minute?"

"That was supposed to be funny," he explained with a toothpick in his mouth.

"It made me sad, it really did."

She led the way into the hotel, her leather bag slung over her shoulder, as the desk clerk looked up and adjusted his glasses with a squirm of his nose. The room had no soul or saving grace, and she displayed it with genuine pride. Her clothes were everywhere as though a valise had exploded. On the dresser he spotted a pint of vodka which she claimed she had bought just for him, though a half inch of it was already gone. She began to undress immediately as Val poured some Smirnoff into a thick water glass, and the phone rang. "Oh, don't answer it," she said with a smirk. "I hate phones. Just leave it ring." Val removed his watch at nine seventeen and dragged it to a stop along the surface of the night table. He found her kneeling beside the bed, her curved spine frail and exposed. "Put in a good word for me," he suggested, making a steady circular motion with his glass and removing the now damp and damaged toothpick from his mouth. In mock seriousness, he began pacing the floor as though dictating to a secretary. "Tell him things haven't been too good lately. In fact, to be specific..." And he related a detailed list of grievances against life. She reached back and tried to wave him into silence. He grinned and continued without a break.

"Oh, really," she laughed, now finished with her prayers. "You're the most disrespectful man I've ever met."

"Well, listen, you're young yet." And just as he had one leg out of his pants the phone rang. This, too, she would not answer, and out of the sheer nonsense of the situation he began to conjugate a European dessert. "*Je flan, tu flanes, il flan, nous flanons, vous flanez, Ils flanent.*"

"What does that mean?" she asked, ignoring the steady ring.

"*Ah, ma petit, flan.* It means I love you in French with a caramel custard."

"I don't get it."

The phone rang again at ten while he was galloping upon her in long strides of mutual passion unable, as before, to bring her to climax. At eleven thirty the phone pulled him from a murky dream in which he was playing tennis against a handball court while ignoring a group of onlookers. At eleven, it rang as he was shaking the last drops of vodka into his mouth, and this time he cursed the sound and all other city noises. It came alive again at twelve thirty while he was deep in a critical evaluation of William Gaddis. (She kept repeating: "I must be stupid. I never even heard of the man.") And as he was making one last assault against her passion, trying to outlive it and bring them both to tranquillity and rest, the phone rang unanswered, at one in the morning, for the last time.

None of this concerned him until he stepped into a phone booth in the West End Bar next evening at ten thirty and phoned her at the hotel. He asked for room 306 and there was no answer. He called again from Ulysses' studio at eleven and still there was no answer. At eleven thirty at The White Horse he rang again to no avail. He phoned at twelve, twelve thirty, one and one thirty. Perhaps this time it was he who was the one at the wrong end of the line, and visions appeared of the squeaking bed going full tilt throughout the night. He cursed her for being the sweet, stupid blonde that she was and for giving him her body instead of what he really wanted: her indifferent, sluggish soul. The next morning after breakfast, in a more dispassionate mood, he relented and phoned her at nine only to be told that she had checked out at eight.

Since Ulysses was off on a field trip that Sunday, Val had to wait until evening to verify what he anticipated was true, that Ulysses didn't know where the hell she was either. Pops was tired and depressed when Val confronted him that night as he sat behind his desk in the studio. His sad face with its crushed leather markings achieved with great strain the amenity of a cordial greeting. The two men spoke quietly, not about Val's concerns (they seemed petty against the despair in these blackened features) but about the Negro's longings to leave the city and retire. That evening the young man's need to withdraw from the free-lance hunt and the old man's desire to sell his business, fused the two of them into agreement. Ulysses locked the studio, and they strolled along Sixth Avenue toward Central Park. The day's heat had darkened the back of his seersucker suit. Val, in knee shorts, with an open-neck sport shirt, paraded alongside with an ice cream pop.

"Well, where do I get the money, tell me? I've got four hundred in the bank and I owe you thirty-five as it is."

"Borrow five hundred and send me the rest as you get it."

He rejected an offer of ice cream and waited for Val's answer. When he said no, Ulysses gave up. His studio was something he had built up over eleven years and it was part of his life. To turn it over to a stranger, for even double the money, sickened him. But as usual he smothered his grief and said nothing more.

They reached the park and crossed over to one of the benches. It was raining so gently that there was no need to take cover. Ulysses sat with his hands folded and looking very much out of place. Beside him, Val lunged forward to keep droplets of vanilla from staining his lap. Gathered beneath the overhang of the Ambassador Hotel, the safe and the wealthy waited patiently while a doorman whistled at the traffic.

"She asked about you, keed."

"Who?"

"She was on the trip today. Tanya."

"Oh?"

"She predicted right. She's a smart girl, that one. She really knows you."

"What in hell are you talking about?"

"I explained how I was trying to sort of con you into buying me out. She said it would never work. Well, she picked it."

"What else she say?"

"Oh, this and that."

"What was it? Spill it!"

"Well, she said—these are her words now—she said you ain't grown up yet. She said if she wanted to predict what you would do, she would just imagine what a child would do and then she would know."

"That bitch." He mouthed the stick clean and it wobbled in his mouth as he spoke. "That pontifical bitch."

Ulysses sat quietly, his suit having contracted measles in the rain.

"Well, she's wrong," Val said, angrily. "Dead wrong."

"About *what?* You takin' the place?"

"No, it so happens she was right about that. But for the wrong reasons."

"I was afraid that's what you'd say."

"Bitch." And Val was afloat for a moment on a high tide of hate.

"Well, I'll just say you returned her regards, huh?"

"Christ, you know something? Now I'm half tempted to buy your goddamned place after all. Just to show that…"

A siren swallowed all other sounds, and Val looked up to see a flashing red bulb as a police car raced by at an angry speed squeezing his heart in the grip of its alarm.

The next time Honey Bea climbed the stairs to Ulysses' studio, she was dressed in a green hip-hugger with matching blouse that displayed a charming midriff of pale belly plus its small, precise button plug. To her surprise she found, entrenched behind the desk, with a hard frown hovering over a yellow sheet of figures, the thin form of Val De Franco. It was a while before she decided he wasn't kidding, that the old place actually had a new owner. It was nothing he said, rather his glued pre-occupation, that convinced her. In fact, he was so absorbed that he didn't even ask where she had been for the last five days or why she had checked out of her hotel in the first place. When she reappeared for work the next evening at seven thirty, she was even more surprised at what she saw. This time everything had been changed. The bare reception room had been turned into a living room, with Val's easy chair and bookshelf oddly out of place against one wall, and his beat-up couch and dresser against the other. In a corner of the back room, or the studio itself, was his enlarger, radio and brass bed. He had obviously moved in to stay.

She liked the idea so much that she moved in with him.

Ulysses Hill remained in the city for a while to sell the furniture in his Harlem apartment. Mostly, though, it was to keep an eye on Val to see how well he took to the problems of private ownership. After a day or two of tacit panic, however, Val seemed to take to them rather well. The main reason was there was very little to do. He would sleep late, receive those, if any, who would rent out the studio by day, and hire two models six nights a week to pose from eight to ten while he sat alone with a drink in the anteroom and read. The only day that required serious planning was Sunday.

Then he would have to rent or borrow four automobiles, buy as many boxed lunches as there were customers and arrange to book two or three models for the day. He would have to drive the lead car to the Willis farm himself and there sit under a tree and read. He kept an advertisement running six times a week in the *Post* and *Telegram*. He did no photo work at all, acquainted himself with most of the figure models in New York and, in a week-and-a-half, had finished two volumes of Durant's *Story of Civilization*. So far, as he told Ulysses, it was a gas.

Living with Honey, however, was something else again. She was both a great help to him and a definite inconvenience. The main problem was that there was too much unscheduled coming and going on her part, and he never knew where she was off to and when she would return. When she did appear, he was certain of only one thing: she would immediately try to drag him off to some gaudy, witless double feature. For such joys, she was insatiable. Perhaps most annoying of all were those continued strange telephone calls made usually in the privacy of a phone booth while Val outside watched her lips through the glass. Occasionally, she would dial the mystery number right in front of him in the studio. However, since her side of the conversation was heavy with cryptic replies and allusions (she kept referring to some amorphic "her") he was left no wiser than before, particularly since she kept insisting that the calls all dealt with that same dying aunt.

Then, ten days after she moved in on him she moved out again. She needed privacy, she said. She wanted her own place where she could think and work. Work at what? She was vague. He found a furnished room for her at Sixteenth Street and Seventh Avenue and she continued to help him with the studio. Frequently she would pose for him without pay, and just as frequently she would round up models at the last minute when he had failed to arrange things himself or was too drunk to know or care.

On the twelfth day after Val took over, Ulysses went south. He refused to let them throw a good-by party for him, made a few quiet farewells and saw Val for the last time beneath the large dome in

Grand Central Station. They faced each other sitting like immigrants on two pieces of luggage. Their conversation dragged. Ulysses finally slapped the young man's bony knee. "Well, buddy, it looks like it's time for me to go. I just want to say I'm crazy about you, keed. It's been great knowing you."

Val slapped the other's knee in return and said nothing.

"And I want to give you some unasked-for advice about the studio."

"You'll *get* your money. Don't *worry* for crysake."

"No, it's not the money. It's about runnin' the place. I just… "

"Damn, you showed me how to run it. You've been explaining procedures to me all week long."

"I know I have, keed. It's just that I want to say… No, listen to me. It's just that I want to say be careful. Really. I mean it. If you start treatin' the whole business lightly, you're going to get in trouble. No, wait a minute. Remember, I've been in this business for eleven years. Longer even. I used to run field trips in Frisco twenty-five years ago, believe it or not. Wait, let me talk. This is a charged situation you're in now. Maybe not for you or the men who pay you, but it's sure as hell explosive for somebody. There's always somebody who's going to try to set a match to it."

Val slid his palm over his cheek as though trying to remember if he had shaved. "What are you trying to say? You're like Eisenhower when the U-2 got shot down. We must all be more vigilant, he said. Me? Vigilant? On a cross-town bus? Vigilant of what? Pops, what are you talking about? What am I specifically to look out for? Huh?"

Ulysses laughed his seductive, surface laugh. He reached out and shook Val's knee as though it were a floor shift in neutral. "Come on, you know what I mean. Just be careful, be sober, be aware. Don't forget dignity, huh, keed?"

"Christ, man, you got to run." Val stood up. "It's almost time. Get going. Get out of here."

"And that Honey. She's quite a fine young… "

"She's a swamp. Stop trying to get me married. Now get out of here. Will ya?"

That slick laugh for the last time. "O.K., keed, I'll stop trying to get you married." He placed both hands on the bone ridges that were Val's shoulders. "So long, keed." And they embraced as though it were a run-through which they would have plenty of time to rehearse and make meaningful, patting each other on the back as though putting out a fire.

Val walked past hollow phone booths and trivial shop windows, the cross-town tide of swinging feet moving him along with the others. He was left with one friend less, and he had failed again to put real meaning into a farewell. He saw imperfectly the first stains of sunset, he saw the great towers dim and blurred, he saw the oncoming faces turn into blobs of color, so full and feverish had his eyes become with tears.

A rhythmic hip, a limp arm lovely against a print dress, suntanned ankles beneath jaunty slacks: these things revived him. On the high note of a bright though sunless sky another vast day concluded as Val drifted along in a state of lonely calm. A monster street scene ensued like an ant hill gone mad. Never had the towers seemed to disgorge so many humans engaging in swift and senseless movement. As Ulysses S. Grant Hill rode away through New Jersey, Val stepped into a sidewalk phone booth. The line buzzed raucously. After buying cigarettes in a nearby drugstore, he went to a phone in back which was marked SORRY, TEMPORARILY OUT OF ORDER. A neighboring phone was occupied. Out in the street, he sprinted toward another booth, but at that moment someone else stepped in. The bar and grill down the block had a wall phone, but all he got was the buzzing again and his dime back. "You talk too damn much, you bitch," said Val to the surprise of a squat old lady sipping beer, and he marched downtown to knock on her door and bawl her out. Rounding the corner of Sixteenth Street, he lit a cigarette, looked up and saw Honey Bea heading toward him, deep in thought, passing close enough for him to have touched her. She's just made one of those goddamn mysterious phone calls, was his first thought, and now she's off to another secret rendezvous. He let the cigarette dangle from his lips. He shifted his eyes. He turned up his collar. Finally, he was in the right mood. All he lacked was a trench coat.

Her blue skirt and peasant blouse descended into the humid IRT alone with a few thousand other people. She stood on the platform and palmed her upswept hair while he watched as best he could from three girders away. Miraculously, she got a seat and rode sideways beneath the city, doubling forward from time to time to dry her forehead with the hem of her skirt. She sat in the jammed car vacant and oblivious, her sandaled feet together, her hands in her lap.

When she didn't get off at Seventy-second Street, he knew he was in for a ride. When she didn't get off at One hundred and twenty-fifth Street, he suspected the whole venture was a big mistake. At One hundred and forty-fifth Street, even he got a seat. At One hundred and fifty-seventh Street she yawned. At Two hundred and seventh Street she scratched her knee. It wasn't until the number 238 sped past on steel girders, slowing down as the train did, that she got up and moved toward the door. He watched her skirt descend into the sunlight where she shifted her feed bag to the other shoulder and with her sandals slapped leather down the street. Three blocks away she made a military left face into an apartment building and disappeared. None of the forty names attached to the forty bells held any meaning for him. He spotted a child's scooter and circled the bare lobby with it several times in playful futility, wandering at last out into the street and down to a candy store on the corner. He ordered a malted milk and considered his worthlessness as a private detective. At last he gave up and headed home. He got no further than the sidewalk outside the store when Honey walked by close enough for him to have touched her. Again she didn't see him, lost as she was in the giggling-googling performance she was putting on for the bundled child in her arms.

When the train paused at Forty-second Street, doors gaping, Val debated getting off and going to the studio. It was now seven, and he had to be back to let in the evening customers at eight. He stayed, however, and with Honey sitting in motherly absorption at one end of the car and with Val holding up an abandoned copy of the *New York Post* at the other, they continued downtown. He trailed her to her building where she disappeared inside. He traced her steps down a dark tunnel, out into a relucent courtyard, up metal steps and into the rear building to confront her door and knock. And knock, and knock until he feared he would get no answer. He was patient. He paused, listening, for she just had to be inside. He went out and hung over the metal railing. Her yellow shade was drawn the length of the window. Scuffling dirt in the courtyard he kept an eye on her eight blank panes of glass. He studied his watch and then a tree as it leaned toward him over an orange wall. He knocked on the door again and on her window as well, for it was getting late and he felt time squeezing him. Unexpected summer breezes bounced a candy wrapper across a rock garden and pushed against Val's face the wing point of his collar. There were no sounds of the city in this brick enclosure nor anything living that he could see. Above him, even the patch of cosmic tent was devoid of color or meaning. Time kept squeezing, yet he stayed for a while and watched as the light began to fade against her blank window.

He met Honey by accident again that night but once more it gained him nothing. Utah De Lux had wangled herself a job singing at an East Side supper club, and for the occasion she wore a black sequined dress with matching eye patch. She asked Val as a favor to photograph her act, and he agreed to be on hand that evening for her midnight performance. Between shows, she and her agent went to a restaurant-bar on top of an office building in midtown where the idea occurred to her to phone Val at the studio and have him join them for a drink. As usual Val arrived late, took the elevator on its long journey to the roof and before he could step out, Utah stepped in.

"Well," she snapped, "if it isn't Old Reliable. Where have you been, Daddy-o? You're late."

"Better late than never."

"In your case, forget it." She turned to her escort, a boy of about twenty-two, who had entered the elevator with her. "Val, I'd like you to meet Raoul, my agent."

"He's your *agent?*"

"Don't bug me, I like 'em young."

"Mr. De Franco," said the boy, "I've been wanting to meet you for years."

"You have?"

"Don't tell me Val owes you money, too?" Utah added.

"When I was young," said the boy, "I had always wanted to be a photographer. I used to follow your work in the magazines. I might even say you were a kind of idol to me. 'Young and brilliant and on his way to the top.' I remember one of the magazines saying that about you. But what happened? Why don't I ever see your stuff around any more?"

Val felt his stomach sink as the elevator hit the ground floor and stopped. He adjusted the camera strap on his shoulder as they walked with the others into the lobby.

"Did I say the wrong thing?" asked the agent, looking from one to the other. "I'm sorry if I did."

"Don't be foolish," Val answered a bit stiffly. "It's a long story."

"And mostly untrue," Utah concluded, grabbing Val's arm. "Come on, we've got to run. Raoul, love ya, baby. Call me. Bye."

To Val's relief, they were soon both in the street waving vainly at passing taxis.

"Guess who I just met up there," Utah said, indicating the rooftop restaurant from which they had both descended. "Little Miss Vacuous."

"Who?"

"Who? Who else? Honey, The Bea."

Utah protested, yet it did no good. Val told her to keep waving for a cab; he'd be right back.

"What's there to see her about so sudden, Daddy-o?"

"It's private."

"Nothing anyone has with you is private."

An excuse occurred to him. He liked it because it was almost the truth.

"I owe her twenty bucks. Long overdue. Be right back, for cry-sake." He dashed off—about ten feet—and good to his word dashed right back. "Say, can you lend me twenty? Until tomorrow?"

"Holy shit. And he says it with a straight face, too."

"You want me to do that shooting tonight, don't you, sweetie-plum?"

"I never learn. I see you coming. But do I call a cop? Do I run and hide? No."

Val bounced on his heels as the elevator rose again to the roof. The questions he wanted to ask Honey about that baby lined up in single file in his mind. At the top floor he stepped out, she stepped in and they met head on.

"Val De Franco, as I live and breathe."

An assortment of sober citizens piled into the car and pushed them to the rear. He saw that now was not the time or place to ask her anything personal. Yet she leaned toward him and whispered a question into his ear.

"Come to my place," she breathed, sending out a whiff of whiskey.

"Can't sweetie-plum. Got a job tonight."

She mocked him with a look of seductive innocence, seeing to it that her breasts remained constantly before him, brazen and peremptory.

"A job. Oh, I bet," she said, no longer whispering. She pushed a stubborn bra strap out of sight.

"No really. It's business. Want to come along?"

"I got to go home. You want to come along?"

"Can't. I told ya."

She acted peeved and stood silent. He reached into his breast pocket for the two tens Utah had given him, but she beat him to it by placing her lips near his ear again.

"Then could you pay me half of that twenty?" she whispered.

"Hey, I was just this minute about to."

He pulled the edges of both bills just far enough out of his jacket pocket for her to see them like the twin points of a handkerchief.

"You lie," she said, mocking him again. "You were not just this minute about to."

He glanced around uneasily at the carload of strangers, all facing the door as though they were damned, and descending without a struggle into hell.

"No, honestly. Utah told me you were here, and so I rushed back up."

There was a faint smile on her lips. "Again you lie. White man speak with forked tongue."

"Look, when we get to the street you can ask her."

"Well, I'm still waiting for that twenty," she whispered into his ear, pretending not to have noticed the money in his jacket. "I really am."

He snatched up the two bills with a flourish of anger and placed them in her hand. Then in a stage whisper, just soft enough for all to hear, he said: "Thank you, my dear, for a wonderful evening."

Her eyes widened at his audacity.

"Shall we say next Wednesday," he continued, "same time, same hotel?"

A few heads had turned to look at her.

"I have some business associates coming to town," he added. "Can you take them on? I'd appreciate it if you'd give them a good price."

"Listen," she said, with a straight face, "tell them I don't do perversions anymore. When I whip you, I do it as a personal favor. But my bursitis has been gettin' worse." She gripped her shoulder. "It really is. Oh, and the next time you want me to watch you ball somebody, no more midgets 'cause that's disgusting."

Now everyone was looking at him instead, and Val's stomach sank again as the elevator came to a halt at the ground floor.

"There you are, you bugger," cried Utah, fixing him with her one visible eye as she stood waiting in the lobby. "Are you coming with me or not?"

"Gladly," said Val, "gladly."

He did find out whose baby it was but not until a good six weeks later. Actually, she was scheduled to appear at the studio the day after he had seen her with the child, and in fact her name was written on the calendar in red ink. It made little difference, however, for she never appeared. Every attempt to get in touch with her by phone failed, and finally he gave up, cursed her, and turned her out of his thoughts. But she was too much a puzzle for him to resist trying to piece it together. Once he remembered Ulysses saying how very clever and bright she was, and in reply he checked to make sure they were talking about the same girl. Then Val explained that he had never seen Honey Bea in other than a state of charming vacuousness. Yet perhaps he had been unfair, for now he had to consider her display of wit in the elevator. Well, that was on the subject of sex, and, come to think of it, he had met many people who could be deft with *double-entendre* and off-colored gags when their minds were otherwise slow and pedestrian. And now he remembered Ulysses once telling him what a fine mimic she was. Again he had checked to make sure they were talking about the same girl. It seemed that Ulysses had overheard her on the phone with a French accent and then again, some days later, he overheard her using a southern drawl. When questioned about it, she proved too modest, said Pops, to admit to any such talent. Val just shook his head. He had never noticed this in her at all. He was certain Ulysses was having illusions.

Two weeks later he began calling again and even made a trip downtown to her door. When he convinced the superintendent to let him in, he found the room sadly silent and stale to the breath. An empty baby's crib was sitting in the tub. By the fourth week he was worried, and by the fifth he was furious. "That half-assed piece of ass," he snarled suddenly in the street one day to the astonishment of a man who was about to ask him directions. "She's forever taking off without a goddamn word to anyone. Well, she can go screw."

At the end of the eighth week she phoned and said she would be in to work the next day. Val was downstairs buying a bottle of gin and the message was taken by Miss Francheska Luca who was there to spend the night. That next evening Honey arrived late, and since she had to rush right into the back room to change, Val discovered only that she had been to California to do film work. Why hadn't she called to let him know? She had left New York suddenly, she said. She had called once but Val was out. Why hadn't she written? She never writes, she explained. It was a peculiarity of hers.

While she posed in front of the hot lights in July heat, Val watched the sweat pour off her body as he waited, seething with a mass of unasked questions. At ten thirty, the fourteen men and the other model finally left. He caught Honey, sheathed again in her clothes and waving good-by, and told her to stay, he wanted to talk to her. He made two drinks and carried them into the back room where she had gone to wait for him. "No," he shouted, placing, almost dropping, the glasses on a nearby table and rushing forward to stop her. "No, no. I just want you to *talk*, to *discuss* something."

"Oh, my mistake," she said, and buttoned up her blouse again.

"That's all right."

"Thought you wanted, you know..."

"Well, perhaps that, too. But right now you sit there quietly on the bed like a good girl and I'll get you your drink, a nice cool gin and tonic, and we'll talk. O.K.? Fine."

But first he had to listen to a rather lengthy tale about how she met Steve Allen in California and how he is going to have her on his TV show in September and perhaps even find a place for her in a movie he was producing.

"Isn't that wonderful news?" she asked.

"I saw you up around Two hundred and thirty-eighth Street with a baby in your arms." He threw the line in quickly and watched her take it right in stride.

"Oh, yes, that's my little niece, Jacqueline. I had just taken her to a doctor for a checkup. Such a cute little thing, she..."

"She's your brother's child?"

"My sister's."

"Your sister lives where?"

"In Jersey."

"And you were taking her there?"

"Yes, to Jersey."

"But you didn't go to New Jersey."

"I said I *was* taking her there. Then I decided not to."

"Why?"

"Not to right away, that is."

"Why?"

"I had to buy something."

"You went to a department store?"

She lifted the glass to her lips, drank a few solemn swallows and lowered the glass to her knee, nodding.

"No, you didn't. You didn't take the child to a department store."

"What day are you talking about?"

"Wednesday, seven weeks ago."

"Oh, I was talking about yesterday."

"Well let's talk about Wednesday, seven weeks ago."

"It sounds like you've been following me, it really does."

"Who knows, maybe I was."

"Were you?"

"Who knows?"

"Well, where did I go? I've never been so cross-examined, really."

"You tell *me* where you went."

"I forget, honest. I really do."

"You went to your own apartment."

"That's right, I remember now. And then I went to Jersey."

"And how much time did you spend in your house before you went to Jersey?"

"An hour?"

"No."

"Two hours? I really don't remember."

"You know what?"

"What?"

"She's your baby, isn't she? You're the mother, isn't that so?"

Sitting on the bed with her legs folded beneath her, she looked at him as though it were still his turn to speak and she were waiting. Her weak, pretty face began to recede from seductiveness, from maturity, from whatever semblance of strength it had.

"Isn't that so?" he asked. "You're the mother, aren't you?"

She waved him away. Then, still staring at him, and without movement or effort, it appeared as though she had set out to disprove his accusation of motherhood by becoming a child herself.

"Well, yea or nay? Which is it?"

She drank in haste, spilling some into her lap and lowering the glass with both hands like a child. Her intense breathing was signaled by the rising and dropping of her breasts. There was not a sound. Then she rose abruptly, letting her drink fall to the bed, its contents spilling like water into sand, and ran to a dark corner of the room. He reached to turn on the overhead bulb, but ignited the flood lamp by mistake. A beam of pure hot light revealed her standing there feeling the plaster as though trying to escape through the wall. Her face, when it turned, was blinded and gashed with tears.

"She's not mine," the girl sobbed. "She's not mine. She's not mine. She's not mine."

Normally he ran out when things got tough, leaving the job or the girl or even the city as though despair, like rain, was something you could get out from under. Yet for the first time in thirty years he was firmly anchored by debt and obligation. This was something new, and when despair touched him he could not run as he once had, he could only laugh or growl, grow flippant or drink.

The beginning of despair, the first of a series of blows, was dealt by the United States Weather Bureau. That is, he was rained out on the first three Sundays in July. For a man who made part of his narrow living on field trips, which he hated, the inclemency cost him dearly; all told, about four hundred and fifty dollars. On the fourth scheduled Sunday, the weather report called for cloudy but clearing, and so Val went ahead, placed the ads and hoped for the best.

Had he only known earlier that Utah, the big bitch, was going to drop out. Had he only checked with her at the beginning of the week as he had promised. So there he was on Saturday evening with the sun going down and only one woman lined up. The phone rang and then there were none. Miss Epps was out. Her roommate called in with the news: Joy Epps had eloped. Hot diggity damn. So there he sat in his studio apartment with his loose-leaf book of professional names opened on his lap and for one and a half hours he made calls. Betty Page. Francheska Luca. Jeanne La Plume, Lolly Brown... on and on. They were either not home, already engaged or not interested. He even called back Utah De Lux. Like a longshoreman she advised him to go screw. As always in a last-ditch emergency he called Honey, and as always in a last-ditch emergency she wasn't home. Hers was the only number he knew by heart: it rang, was ringing, had rung. This repeated itself until finally he hung up with a slam and charged down the stairs to the pavement where the street lights winked on in sad greeting. Unrolling his left sleeve, heading nowhere, yet toward the subway, he passed a quartet of girls singing "Everybody Loves Saturday Night."

Ten minutes later at West Eighth Street, Val emerged sweating from the subway, cursing its hothouse intensity. He wandered upstream through a girl-boy crowd, and from each slim ankle up to each lovely face his spirits climbed with his gaze. Then he would remember Sunday, and they would fall again. "TWO BEAUTIFUL MODELS," said the advertisement. Yet so far he had none, and he hated the whole business. The bar was like a crowded elevator. He rammed his way in, bought a Ballantine ale and decided to try Honey once again. Two trips to the phone booth found it occupied, first by a tall Ivy Leaguer who kept the door open and stood with one foot on the seat, and second by a disheveled Village type who kept twisting a strand of hair and nodding as she talked. He came back twice more and she was still there, as though settled for the night. Val knocked on the glass. "They just fired on Fort Sumter," he said, when she opened the door. "Very funny, my good man," she replied, her chin needing a shaving, and shut the door on him again. "Nobody's patriotic any more," he complained to a redhead who squirmed her way past and nodded to humor him.

When the booth was finally abandoned, he jumped in and found it the roomiest place in the bar. As he reached for the phone it rang and for an instant he was paralyzed as though the ground rules of life had become reversed.

"Hello?"

"Hello," said a young woman's voice and again he was paralyzed, for it sounded so much like Honey. "Would you please see if Hyman Lowe is at the bar?"

"You serious with that name?"

"Please, he's my husband."

Val leaned out into the congealed mass, hesitated, then decided, "What the hell," and cried loudly: "*Hyman Lowe? Is Hyman Lowe here?*" No one even looked his way.

"He's either not here, Mrs. Lowe, or afraid to come forward."

"Thank you." Click.

Val dialed, Honey didn't answer, and he fought his way back to his evaporating glass of ale and to the blonde who had occupied his place at the bar.

"Val De Franco," she said, pointing her full blouse at him, "as I live and breathe."

She kissed him and then introduced the three men who were with her. "This is Knox, Cox and Fox," she said, indicating each in turn. "Actually Knox Schuster, Fred Cox and Joe Fox. But I like them better when they rhyme." She buried her nose in a Scotch on the rocks and winked at Val over the rim.

"I just now called your place. Are you free tomorrow… the field trip?"

"Honey needs the money. Yes, I'm free. I was going to call you myself, but I figured you for being booked. Somebody drop out, sweetie?"

"Everybody dropped out. What about your friend Lona?"

"Atlantic City. She and some divinity student."

"What about the girl you worked with at the Coliseum? The one who hates Turks."

"The Negro girl?"

"No, the one who claims she slept with Antony Armstrong-Jones."

"Oh, big Bertha. No, sweetie, she doesn't do that kind of work."

"What sort of field trip," asked Knox Schuster, leaning in like a bodyguard.

"The Negro girl then?" Val suggested, placing the cool glass against his cheek.

"She's out of town for an abortion."

"Well, that's that."

"Let me see, who could I get for you?"

"What kind of field trip," asked Knox Schuster.

"Don't you think this one looks like Dana Andrews?" asked Honey.

"At least," said Val, lifting his drink.

She patted Knox on the cheek. "You should be in the movies, you really should."

"I've heard that line before," said Val, and Honey gave him a playful shove.

"What kind of field trip?" said Knox Schuster.

Honey looked so innocent she appeared retarded. "My, you are persistent."

"Well, I've got to go find me another girl," said Val.

"Wish I could help you, sweetie."

"Just be there at nine."

"I may be a bit earlier," she suggested, kicking him gently.

"Come on," said Knox Schuster. "What kind of field trip?"

Val was out in the street hurrying in no particular direction and with Sunday's commitment still squarely on his mind. In another bar he drank straight Jack Daniels and tugged at the front of his shirt to fan himself. Somewhere between the third and fourth drink an idea caught hold. There was one last girl he could call. One he hadn't thought of. He pushed her out of his mind. In a drugstore he made more calls to a few of the girls who hadn't been home the first time, found them still not home and went to another bar. He ran through whole chapters of his past for girls he might have missed, but he kept coming back to the same one, and the idea of calling her grew. His memory brought back film clips from a time six months past when he and she were joined in a separate-but-equal love. He fell into a reverie, reliving moments of merriment that now in retrospect took on a fullness and near-perfection they never had. He consumed another drink, damned his whole crowded past and, to escape thought, pushed himself into a barroom discussion of Cuba, Richard Burton, and high rents.

Val found himself walking up Sixth Avenue at Twenty-third Street and carrying a half pint of vodka. He was trudging happily through an undergrowth of inebriation thinking great thoughts which he immediately and lavishly forgot. The bottle landed noisily on the wooden floor, and he found himself awake at the studio on his couch realizing that he had been asleep for God knew how long. A neon bulb outside his window alternated between igniting the room with morose flames of red and hiding it in darkness. He rose as though from the grave and turned on a light which made a soft metallic noise and went dead. Another lamp didn't work at all. He struck a match, knelt on the floor, dialed the number and fell into darkness again. Her phone rang in the same frequency as the neon light. His watch said twelve thirty-five. A passing convertible sent up a flurry of loud jazz. Her phone rang three times and then was answered. But not by a voice; by a semisilence of wire-twisting, adjusting, arranging and hand fumbling. Then came the remembered voice in all its familiar multitoned, actress-rich loveliness.

"Ah, *shit*. It spilt … Hello?"

"Hello."

"Damn, it's over everything."

"What is?"

"I knocked over a drink. Tsh. Wait a minute. Hang on. Oi vay."

Silence. Then after much movement: "Hi. Still there?"

"I'm still here, Tanya."

"*Oui*, like the whole bed's wet."

"Stop kretching."

"It's *kvetching*. Not kretching. Christ, what a lousy Jew you'd make."

"Or Christian too, for that matter."

"Who *is* this? Is this Mike?"

"Who in hell is Mike, for crysake?"

"Val," she said in soft surprise. "Val. You sound so much like Mike. I never realized it before."

"Who?"

"Mike Ferrero. My agent."

"Damn it, I thought you were dropping him."

"Well, I was, but then he began getting me jobs and all. Val, how *are* you?" Then, in a neutral voice that was meant to reveal nothing, she unknowingly crawled through the receiver and into his bloodstream with: "It's been a *long* time."

They indulged in cautious conversation that delved none too deeply and revealed next to nothing. Abruptly, Tanya ended it.

"Val, I'd love to continue, but I can't talk now."

"Oh, you're not alone?"

"Kind of, like, that's it, yeh."

"A woman, no doubt."

"Other," she said, missing his sarcasm.

"Call you back later tonight?"

Silence.

"No good?" he asked.

"Accurate."

"Listen, I'm doing different work now."

"I know. I heard you took over Pop's studio."

"As luck would have it. Hey, how would you like to take a nice ride into the country tomorrow with a whole bunch of strangers and myself, commune with nature, enjoy the great outdoors, and take your clothes off?"

"What happened? You short a girl this weekend? Another job of planning well done?"

"She eloped, for crysake. I couldn't help it."

"Ah, huh."

"What do you say, Slim?"

As they talked, he realized with mixed feelings the degree of reconstruction that had been completed in her life. It was as though she had never shared his passion, as though, in fact, the very memories of their intimacy had been removed from her mind by surgery.

She said she would do it. She would come on Sunday because her dentist, her landlord, her grocer, her analyst, her dramatic coach were all more or less on her neck.

"Have to run now," she said. "Like we've got to schlepp up to Harlem to catch Ella Fitzgerald. Thanks for calling, Val. Honest ingin."

"Tomorrow at nine?"

"Honorable number one daughter ah no forget."

The twentieth century surrounded him again with its electric razzmatazz. The neon light sent its raw flames through the Venetian bars while the refrigerator groaned, the sink dripped, and the toilet gurgled. He savored the memory of her marvelous voice, and wondered whom she was with. Well, at least they were going out. It appealed to his devilish soul that she would be spending Sunday with him and that Honey would be there too, and that neither would know about the other. He laughed at this, felt hungry and then lonely and found himself opening a new bottle. He sat with his drink in a dark, dusty corner of the solar system and tried to find comfort in his own voice. "'And on Seesaw Sunday nights I wooed whoever I would with my wicked eyes.' " Then he discovered himself in bed dreaming that he had gotten up in the middle of the night to answer the door only to find in a surprising revelation a moment later that it was Honey and not a dream he had had.

Daylight pierced his brain. He heard the phone jarring him.

"It's morning, boobie. Up wake."

"Hoigis?" He cleared his throat. "Who is this?"

"Oh, heavy, heavy hangs the hangover over your head."

"Tanya?"

"Dat's-a-me."

"What time is it?"

"Eight-thirty."

"Christ."

"Do me a favor? Sweetheart? Pick me up at an address I'll give you, O.K.? Broadway, in the eighties only. Like I'm not home now. It'll save me all kinds of tzurus. I won't have to schlepp downtown and all. It's on your way anyway, huh? Baby? Apartment 5C. Pressa da five-a-see. I come-ah right down."

"You slept over at some guy's place?" he asked, frowning. It was out before he could catch it.

"Can you, huh, baby?"

In the foyer he could find nothing but a stubby pencil hanging from a string at the bulletin board. Angrily he snapped it free, bringing the entire board crashing to the floor. "Screw you," he said and re-entered the studio to discover Honey Bea sitting up naked in the bed he had just left.

"Last night," she babbled excitedly, "do you know what you did?"

"Wha?"

"You don't remember?"

"No, what? Horrors. What?"

"You passed out, I mean it. You passed right out right on top of me."

"O.K., shoot. What's the address?" he said to the phone.

INTERVIEW

ELIZABETH Street, in the Italian section of Manhattan, often resembles a three-ring circus where, all at once, one can find a rousing stick-ball game, a truck-mounted merry-go-round and an unleashed fire hydrant for beachless children. In the middle of the block on the fourth floor of a walk-up tenement building in a twenty-dollar-a-month cold-water flat we confronted Val De Franco in bare feet drinking a gin and tonic. At first glance, his apartment looks more like a storage room than someone's living quarters. An Omega B2 enlarger, like some strange Martian lamp, stands between the couch and the worktable. Close by is a painting in cubist style, of Christ on the cross but with real wooden spikes driven into his palms and through the canvas and into the wall. Everywhere else one looks there are photographs, all bleed-mounted and of various sizes. A shot of a paint-chipped keyhole, through which can be seen the blurred outline of a distant tree, is the size of a postcard. A child's arm holding aloft cotton candy is on a four-foot-high, six-inch-wide print. There are laughing women's faces and thoughtful, somber men. There are stunning nudes and comic self-portraits and there is that lovely prizewinner of some years back entitled "On the Bed" which shows a woman's face in profile kissing the inside of a man's elbow.

Seated in the center of this impressive display is its creator, a lean energetic man with straight, unruly hair, clear, cat-gray eyes and a perpetual expression of light mockery. Of the five young photographers selected at our request, by a committee of photo editors, as being the most promising on the American scene, De Franco lives in the worst surroundings, has done the least work of late and was the one who most wanted to discuss topics unrelated to his field. He made another round of drinks, sprawled on the couch, encouraged us to "have at it" and then began conducting the interview himself.

VAL: Isn't the neighborhood great this time of the day? It's a Breughel with touches of Hieronymus Bosch. But you should come down during the festival. The streets are strung with lights, and we even have our own Ferris wheel. Local Carusos are forever singing Puccini with half-ass amateur orchestras sawing away behind them, while the bedworthy Italian chicks are all dressed up to kill and maim. It's just great. The best of all is at six in the morning when they pull a statue of the Virgin through the streets. The first time I saw it I thought, surely everyone is asleep. Yet, out of each doorway steps a well-dressed Italian who pins a five – or a ten-dollar bill on the statue and then disappears. You must come down to see it. Don't forget.

INTERVIEWER: That's the Festival of Saint Padua you're describing. Didn't you do a picture story on that?

VAL: Two, in fact, and three on the Chinese New Year. Now there *is* a great one. Ever see it? You should. New York has some great events that few people know or care about. But you don't want to talk about *this* now do you? You want to discuss *f*/ openings and film speeds and that kind of crud. Or how I got into photography? *(Laughing.)* Something inane like that?

INTERVIEWER: That'll do fine as a starter.

VAL: How did I get started in this racket? Well, first I took up acting. I left Nashville and went to Chicago and became an actor. Worked here and there. Did O.K. and dropped it for painting. Great fun, painting. I was big on cubism and all that. Here in New York I had a few showings. Got reviewed fairly well and then dropped it. One day I sold a painting for two hundred dollars to this rich creep in Mamaroneck whose check bounced. He didn't answer my letters so I hitched up there to see him. He was friendly. Gave me a drink. All apologies. I just knew I wasn't going to get a cent out of the bastard. Then the doorbell rang and when he left me to answer it, I grabbed the only expensive thing in sight and high-tailed it out the back. I ran twelve blocks to the railroad station where the only thing moving was a line of freight cars. I hopped it and rode straight to Albany. It took me two days to get back to New York but I didn't care because I was the proud owner of a brand-new contraband Rolleiflex. You sure you don't want another drink?

INTERVIEWER: Your success was immediate. Several first and second prizes and a number of fine picture stories made you into a man of promise. Outstanding was that bleak documentary you did on Bellevue Hospital and that poetic series on an interracial marriage. Our committee ranks you among the most promising and least known talents in the business. But about a year ago you became less and less active in art photography. Would you care to comment on that?

VAL: No, I wouldn't. But I guess I'll have to. I've been told that I'm flighty. That I lose interest too easily. That I get bored. But people don't understand. It's a matter of freedom from technique. In most art forms, to reach your potential you must master techniques. That takes a long time, and it doesn't guarantee that you have any potential at all. Anais Nin has great technique but she's nowhere as a writer. Rimski-Korsakov was one of the greatest technicians in music. Jerry Lewis, one of the greatest technicians in comedy. So what? Nothing. Innocent though it may be, I was looking for an art form where technique was not important. Photography was it, or so I thought.

INTERVIEWER: Then why did you leave?

VAL: I got bored.

INTERVIEWER: Then, without technique, art fails to retain its challenge. Is that what you're saying?

VAL: Hell, I'm not saying that at all. I just lost interest. You sure you don't want another drink? Got plenty.

INTERVIEWER: So you're doing commercial work now just to make a living. You've given up the art side of it for good?

VAL: Right now I'm kind of hung up on the cinema. I'd love to get into that. I don't know where I could steal a motion picture camera, though, do you? Presents a problem.

INTERVIEWER: One of your colleagues has this to say about you, and I quote. "He has developed self-destructiveness to a fine art. He has ability without tenacity. In America we have the phenomenon of the ever-promising artist who never fulfills his promise. De Franco is the epitome of this. He is perennially promising and that, I think, is about the sum of it."

VAL: That's hard to say, isn't it? Perennially promising. Perennially promising. Some quote, though. Wow. He really must be jealous, the bastard. Got any more?

INTERVIEWER: All right. One of the top cheesecake models in this city has this to say: "Val is the least inhibited man I've ever met. Sometimes when he's with a woman he'll do in public what the average man wouldn't do in private. He's a kind of comic virtuoso of immorality. Yet there is something fresh and new about him. He's good to be with because he's the only real man-child I've ever met.

VAL: Got any more? Those are great. Comeoncomeon. Some more.

INTERVIEWER: Don't you have any comment to make in return?

VAL: What can I say? They're right, I'm right. We're *all* right. That's the beauty of controversy. Everybody's right. Someone thinks I'm worthless. Someone thinks I'm worthwhile. They're both correct. That last quote, the one from the broad with the hot pants. I don't know who she is, but I do hope I did right by her. Sounds like I didn't, though, despite all her comments about evil. Means I passed up a good thing and didn't know it. Drat! Come on. More quotes. Comeoncomeoncomeon.

INTERVIEWER: This next one is a bit different. It's not about you but about your line of work. A British critic said recently that all film art is limited because it is forced to deal with reality. Do you agree?

VAL: You're de*ter*mined to trap me into a serious discussion, aren't you? All right, let's see. All art is limited because it's forced to deal with critics. Hell, one man's reality is another man's myth. For me a cameraman doesn't have to transplant a nose or twist trees to earn the title of artist. Some photographs are as vivid and meaningful to me as the Egdon Heath of Thomas Hardy, or Picasso's "Winter Landscape" or Respighi's "Pines of Rome." For example, W. Eugene Smith's *The Thread Maker*, or Edward Weston's *Rock Erosion*, or David Douglas Duncan's *Marines, Korean War*, or many of those early great Stieglitz things. Christ! Great, great stuff. Sure photography is limited. So is music but in a different way. Yet photography goes as directly to the heart, is as universal and possibly more eternal. And it's not true that any amateur can take a great shot. What slander! Theoretically, I suppose, it could happen. But I've never seen it happen. To the non-photographer it seems all so simple. You know, snap and wind, snap and wind until the end of the roll. Nonsense. Look at the way Margaret Bourke-White had to struggle and reshoot and reshoot those relatively simple steel mill night shots. Or try, just try, to capture a mountain the way Ansel Adams does. Or try to reproduce a *Vogue* high-fashion shot. Then you'll see what technique really means. Or wander through a race riot or a revolution with things flying all around you and let's see if you or *any* amateur can get results the way a *Life* staff pro does. You'll more than likely just get your head smashed. You need timing, selectivity, technique, experience and courage. Only when you've tried it can you know how very easy it's not. Many people think that writing is easy. Hell, I can write, they think. I know a language, I've lived a little and so—pouff—I'm a writer. Ha, what bilge, I'd like a dime for every novel that was conceived but never attempted, attempted but never finished,

finished but never published, published and even well received but then was, after all, a total piece of crap. Well, for one man to achieve a backlog of great or even fine photographs, with originality, feeling, style and technique, let me tell you, man, it's a bone-breaker. Frankly, I'd rather try a novel. Snap-wind, snap-wind. Bullshit. Now there, you see how pompous one gets with these damned serious questions? Jesus, I'm going to make another drink. You sure you don't want one?

INTERVIEWER: Perhaps you'll allow me just one last serious query which we ask everybody? Could you tell me what it is you want from life?

VAL: Boy, you dig up dillies, don't you? Well, let's see, what do I want? Money, laughter and Tina Louise. And I'd love to give Grace Kelly a real pinch. You know, for old times' sake. I'd like to have a steady income from a trust fund so I could slump down in a corner of some Parisian bar and drink myself silly and let the rest of the world go screw. Joyce said that he should be supported by the state because he was capable of enjoying life. That goes for me, too. What do I want from life? Beginnings. A lot of beginnings. With women, ideas, trips started, projects begun. Beginnings are the best. Oh, and I want a perversion named after me. The De Sade bit. De Francoism. De Francoistic. Perhaps it'll mean the acquiring of sexual gratification by abandoning an art form. Who knows? Perhaps the only complete act I've ever committed was leaving home. Definition: De Francoism: the traveling from Nashville to New York and no farther.

INTERVIEWER: Why did you leave Nashville?

Val: To avoid killing my father. Actually, I didn't live in Nashville. I lived in a tiny town miles away. My father owned the local butcher shop. We should have been well off, only he was a cheap son of a bitch. He had three children. I was the youngest, and we were all forced into the butcher business. Even my sister chopped up meat for a while. My mother was a floor mat, weak and ineffectual. My father used a whip. A real tyrant. Eli (my big brother) wanted to study art, but the old man was against it. One day he broke into the store-house where Eli kept all his paintings and burned them. Eli just kept on painting and my father just kept on burning. One day Eli painted a canvas of a man who was hanging dead by the neck from a rafter inside an empty church. The painting was standing above the fireplace when my father came home from work. He didn't touch it. He always wanted Eli to be present before burning a canvas. We all waited for Eli to come home. But he was already home. He was in the cellar hanging from one of the rafters. Seventeen years old. When my sister Edwina was eighteen she fell in love with an actor who wanted to marry her. She got beaten at home whenever she dated him, and finally the old man broke up the romance completely and made her marry some local jerk. It turned out to be a disaster, and Edwina wanted out but, with a series of mysterious threats, which I never understood, good old Dad forced her to stay in it. You see, he was concerned with the family name. Finally, of course, she ran away and we have never heard from her since. A year later I tried to run away myself. I was fifteen at the time.

On four different occasions I tried to escape to Nashville, and each time, with the help of the police, Dad caught me. He would bring me back and beat the living daylights out of me, and each time I would begin making plans to try again. The bus and railroad depots had been alerted to look out for me. So one day I quietly left town as a stowaway in the back of a hearse. A week later I was in Chicago. On the fifth try I had made it. I remember that day. It was raining its ass off, and I was wet and broke and scared shitless. But there was one thing I had learned. Man, there was one thing I did know. I knew that anywhere, any place was better than home any time. You get to know those things. I had the pleasure of learning it real fast.

SHE discovered herself awake, knowing that she had been awake for a while without realizing it. As the world slipped into place she lay on her back feeling small and insignificant. She noticed the empty bottle of Smirnoff and the thick water glass beside it. She remembered now that she was on East Twenty-third Street, and the hotel room closed in on her in drab finality. Someone else was in the bed as well. She didn't bother turning to see who it was. Mornings were never easy: they were heavy, sharp-edged, slow and without promise. The evenings were different; they seemed stored up with possibilities and waiting for her to make an appearance.

She escaped into the bathroom where her body faced her in the mirror with dumb disapproval. The shower curtain had a disturbing smell. The water cleansed her. The towels mothered her. Her cosmetics altered her, and she remembered how Liz Taylor awoke in the beginning of *Butterfield 8*. Yet the terrible feeling of morning didn't dissolve.

When she reappeared, he was already dressed and trying to squeeze that final drop from the pint of vodka. Now she even remembered the night before: the hamburgers he bought for her and the movie with Rock Hudson and Doris Day. She wasn't vacant any longer. She was playing the role of Honey Bea as it had evolved in Val's presence. Yet she wasn't quite up to it, and so she waited for the room to be empty of him, though it would make her empty as well. A kiss and a closed door and she was finally free to be nothing.

Hollywood melodrama was, as usual, her guidebook, and with it she created any number of Honey Beas moving in and out of them, one after the other, to meet whatever challenge, to adapt to whatever conditions that threatened to expose the very blankness which she was now, for a while, allowing herself to feel. Performing so many Honey Beas was exciting, exhausting and even frightening, for once she displayed one of her characters to somebody it had to be maintained for as long as that person knew her, and two such people knowing two such divergent Honey Beas could not be allowed to meet her at the same time. Usually she would adopt a role when there was someone present, but sometimes, when she became particularly lonely or lost, she would perform for herself and, on occasion, invent someone to perform to, as well.

This morning, the act of assembling herself into the bits and pieces of her clothes seemed a task beyond her strength. She wished life was more like the movies where trivia and pointless repetition were skipped completely. It took her an hour just to begin the ritual of dressing. But once out in the sunlight, she safely became someone else again. As she waited at the bus stop, a young man came by, glanced at her, and went on his way. He wore a nineteenth-century beard and almost no hair on top of his head. His face, however, surrounded as it was by the accouterments of age, was clearly that of a twenty-year-old boy.

"You know what y'all look lack?" she said, "Y'all look lack Dr. Brown's cough drops goes to college."

"I was hoping you'd like the beard?" she imagined him answering.

"Ah do. But it makes you look lack a cala youth. Except ah don't know what cala means."

She was most glamorously dressed (hair up, earrings glistening), and he escorted her with obvious pride. He paid for her on the crosstown bus and he had two tokens ready for the IRT.

"You look very good," he said above the roar of the train.

"Why, ah thank you, sir."

"You know something. I've known you now for a month and a half, and I still don't know anything about you. I mean, I know you came from the South and all that. Nashville, right?"

"Memphis, sweetie."

"I mean, what was your childhood like? You know, briefly."

She made a grimace at the ceiling fan as it fluttered the edges of her hair. Patting herself on the head, she turned and reluctantly related the history of her life. She was, as she had once told him, an orphan. Her father, a member of the Lincoln Brigade, had been killed in Spain on the day she was born. Three years later her mother lost her life when the stove in their Memphis apartment exploded. Honey, her sister and brother were raised by their grandmother who taught them all to be prim and proper ladies and gentlemen. Honey both loved and hated the South and finally came to New York when she was seventeen to live for a while with an aunt in the Bronx. It was then she learned that a wealthy relative had left her a hundred thousand dollars to be awarded to her in full on her thirtieth birthday. In other words she would be rich in exactly five years.

"How did you get the baby?" he wanted to know.

"That was easy. Ah slept with a mayen."

He stared at her, and then his young lips moved in the beard. "Who was he?"

"He was ma legal husband. He was a poet. We had an apartment in Brooklyn Heights overlookin' the water. The very same one Tom Wolfe once had. We lived there for a year."

"Then, what happened?"

"He disappeared. He clean disappeared. Ah really mean it. He went out walkin' late one nyut. He did that often so he could kana recharge his muse. Ah called the police and everythang but he just never came byeck."

"You poor kid."

"He was never found. That was almost two years ago."

"How you must have suffered."

"Ah tried to kill myself twace."

"You poor kid."

At Two hundred and thirty-eighth Street, they walked hand in hand toward a large ugly building at which point she made him dissolve into thin air. Fat mothers in bargain-sale dresses sat on folded chairs and watched her approach while she in turn watched the blue sky and the windowboxes and the bargain-sale dresses and a few little ones on quick tricycles ringing their bells grimly as she paraded into the building.

When the glamorous Miss Bea made her next appearance, she was carrying little Jacqueline in a pink blanket, and the fat mothers watched the showgirl diminish toward the corner; and if not a showgirl then a model (except she wasn't carrying a hatbox) or perhaps a call girl (except she had a baby), and what apartment had she visited? and whose daughter or wife or mistress or niece or friend was she anyway? for they couldn't remember seeing the likes of her around here ever before.

On their way downtown, the young man with the beard was there again, wheedling out of her stories about her movie-making experiences. Rocking the baby in her arms, she talked about the film people she had met or worked with: Mickey Rooney, Tony Perkins, Kim Hunter and Paul Newman. Then she spread some of the latest gossip and finished by reeling off a comprehensive list of Hollywood homosexuals.

At One hundred and sixteenth Street, she dismissed him but, to Honey's annoyance, he persisted in his request to accompany her on her first job of the day. She exerted a slight effort of will, however, and once and for all made him dissolve on the spot.

With a slip of paper in her hand, she entered the lobby of a riverside apartment building and waited in the plush silence as the floor numbers above the elevator door lit up in reverse sequence.

A clipped poodle and a stagnant old lady minced out and headed toward the sunlight as Honey, surveying her own image in a hand mirror, ascended to the twelfth floor.

"You're late but lovely," said Brian, who kissed her cheek and led her into the living room. "Check the pad. High class, no?"

"It's all right. Whose is it?"

"Belongs to a cat I know. How 'bout a drink?" Then screaming: "*Hey, Tunney, she's here!* Scotch? You're lookin' wicked, kid."

"And you're as smooth as ever."

"How's Jacqueline?" he asked, glancing at the baby.

"Why? You want to be her daddy again?"

"Is that old black whore still taking care of her?"

"That old black whore," said Honey, receiving the drink from him, "happens to be a lifesaver to me and a dear sweet person."

"I didn't mean…"

When the door to the bedroom opened and a policeman stepped out, Honey stiffened.

"This is Tunney," said Brian with a malicious smile, "I think you two had better get acquainted."

Making Tunney a refill, he accidentally dropped some cigarette ashes into the drink. Looking to see if anyone had noticed, Brian scooped them out again with his fingers.

Honey was lost in the act of ignoring the policeman. She yelped as the host slapped her on the rump. "Relax, he's no cop. He's a plot salesman at Forest Lawn."

"Don't slap me there. I don't like it."

"All right, all right. We're all friends, O.K.? Down the hatch."

Tunney, who had been inspecting the blonde with a total lack of expression, brightened as he waved a sports magazine at the host.

"You know who holds the slugging championship in the whole history of the National League?"

"You ready to earn some bread?" Brian asked her.

"That's correct, sir."

"Who takes care of the kid?"

"She'll behave."

"In all of baseball, who has the top slugging average in the N.L.? Come on, give a guess."

"What's the story line, anyway?" Honey wanted to know.

"Right here, read it." Brian handed her a piece of yellow graph paper with several paragraphs typewritten across it.

She sank into the couch, the baby in her arms, and placing her drink on the rug, read the page while Tunney jabbed Brian's arm with the rolled magazine.

"No," he snapped, "I do not know who holds the slugging average."

"What does 'elusive' mean?" she asked, without looking up.

"It's Willie Mays," said Tunney, smiling triumphantly. "Old Say Hey, himself. How about that?"

"Can't be true," said Brian.

"Can't be true?" she asked. "That way the sentence doesn't make sense."

"It's written right here, wise guy," said Tunney, with a vengeance, "it's written right here."

"'Elusive' means heard to get hold of, hard to find," said Brian. "Somethin' like that."

"I told you Mays is a great ballplayer."

"Tunney, are you ready to start shootin' or not?"

"Yeh, what are you gettin' sore about?"

"What does 'repentant' mean?" Honey asked.

"Well, get your hat on and let's get ready."

"My hat's inside. I'm ready," Tunney replied with injured flatness.

"I want to get this done in one shooting."

"I ain't holding you up none."

"Well, when our *star* gets ready," said Brian, sarcastically.

"What does 'tumultuous' mean?" Honey asked without looking up.

Finally, Brian got both of them into the bedroom where a Bolex was mounted on a tripod, and two floodlights were ready to be turned on. A cardboard replica of a wall safe hung from a nail. Brian instructed them in the roles they were to play. Tunney pulled his hat on and looked the perfect picture of one of New York's Finest, except that his badge read DEPUTY SHERIFF BGD SAN FRANCISCO. Honey was at the mirror again, and she saw Brian's image with his low-brow, con-man's face giving her the eye. Tunney had to be told to put away his sport magazine. Honey was handed a raincoat which she put on, cinching the belt. When, to kill time, Tunney took a full swing at an imaginary three and two pitch, Brian told him to cut it out and get into the closet. Honey tried on a black mask with diamond-shaped eyepieces as in the film *The Mark of Zoro*. She stepped out into the living room again and turned up the collar of her coat. As she waited, she made faces at Jacqueline who lay quietly in the chair.

Hearing her named called, Honey entered in character and, without intending to, squinted at the astonishing lights which were now baking the room. "Skulk," said Brian from behind the purring camera, "Skulk." She hunched over and exaggerated an evil, secret tiptoe movement across the room. "Look around occasionally," he ordered, his cigarette dropping ashes as he spoke. Honey fingered the combination of the imitation wall safe, looking over her shoulder occasionally like a born thief. Further instructions were shouted from across the room. The closet opened, and out stepped police officer Tunney, gun in hand, and pressed it quickly into the small of her back. In wild-West style, she reached for the sky, and to the best of her acting ability squinted in full-scale terror which the mask mostly concealed. After making her turn around, Tunney removed the black cloth from her face and discovered, to his exaggerated theatrical surprise, a very pretty girl. A few prods from his gun forced her to remove her coat as well, at which point the police officer pantomimed pleasure at finding such a lovely creature his captive. Next, it was time out to reload the camera.

"I have to make a sissy," Honey said.

When all was ready again, she resumed her state of captivity (closer to the center of the room, this time) and began begging the officer not to arrest her. "Tunney, baby, now smile lustfully. Good. Now say something to her. Just move your lips. Good. Now, Honey, show you know only too well what he wants. Good." She followed his instructions blindly acting at being an actress and hoping against hope that she might possibly be the great undiscovered talent of her time. The policeman insisted that she remove other articles of clothing. With seductive reluctance, she was finally made to take off her black dress and, after more of his threats, her shoes and stockings as well. This will all be over soon, she told herself. Just do it, and that's that. Just get it over with. Seated now on the bed, half blinded by the lights, all she could make out was the tall blue figure of the law pointing the revolver at her. Soon off came her bra. He shook the gun in her face one last time, and then there she was completely naked in the bleaching lights and the constant eye of the spinning camera. She thought only of the money this would earn her, and she hoped that he (behind the camera) would choke from watching and wanting her. Now the cop was on the bed, as well, with his weight and his onion breath and his bleak flesh, and she imagined herself in Val's arms instead. She gave forth with a dead imitation of lust while behind the camera, directing her, watching her, was the father of her little child. Savagesavagesavage kept exploding again and again in her mind and her body poured sweat, staining the silk counterpane on which she worked.

This time the fat mothers in the bargain-sale dresses seated on folding chairs in front of the old apartment building recognized her immediately. Dressed in sandals and a peasant blouse and skirt, with her blond hair loose, her face friendly and without makeup, she was "that woman" they had seen several times before, the one who came with the baby to 6D and then left again. By now they guessed that she had a sister who she sometimes sent to fetch the baby in her place; a glamorous lady, much older, who dressed in expensive jewels with her hair high on her head and who once arrived in a cab, noticeably drunk, with the child in her arms.

Honey swept past them and trudged on up to the top floor and into 6D. Bedlam at once. Two mulatto children grabbed her legs while one cried from a nearby crib and a fourth in a highchair banged his spoon. Their Negro mother, ugly, smiling with a front tooth prominently missing, appeared from the kitchen with the haggard look of an experienced field general in midbattle. Honey distributed hellos and kisses until she was able to get away, alone, into one of the bedrooms. She tiptoed across the floor and peeked cautiously into the crib. Jacqueline, lying motionless on her back and seemingly in tune with the mood of secrecy and silence all around her, stared up at her mother with furtive interest. Unable to restrain her love, Honey lifted the child to kiss and cherish her. "How's my fat old lady? My beautiful fat old lady. Huh? Huh? Oh, I could eat her up. Oh, I could eat her up. Oh, I could eat her up." One role Honey didn't have to playact was that of a mother. In fact, she was almost afraid of her love, as though if she unleashed it all at once upon her adorable child, the very abundance of it might kill.

"Why don't you tell 'im you have a baby and be done with it?" said the Negro woman with the missing tooth. They were facing each other across the kitchen table, Honey looking sixteen again and holding Jacqueline in her arms. "Don't you think it's silly, child? And why do it? 'cause I can't keep her *all* the time. I'm sorry. I am sorry 'cause I know it's tough on you when you ain't got a place to leave her. But the old man is complainin' about my workin' too hard already. Anyway, I'm not her mother. You are. If you care for this guy—what's his name, De Franco?—tell 'im. You do care for him. I know it, so don't bull me. You care for him, yes you do."

Honey spoke in a tone of light sadness. "Ah, *oui*. I am *thinking* about heem very off-on. Before I had Jacqueline I thought ne-vair, ne-vair I could love anyone. Then I find I love ma ba-be. Ah, yes, about heem I think very off-on."

"So tell 'im, woman. You have a baby. Tell 'im. Big deal."

Honey slipped a look at her child. "No, I cannot."

"Jesus, child, *why?*"

Honey looked as if she were being reprimanded by her mother and said nothing.

"I know what it is. You're afraid if you tell 'im he'll skip on ya. Ain't that it? He'll run out, and again you'll be left with a baby and no man."

Honey nodded, though not really in agreement. For a moment there was a flurry of noise in the apartment. Children crying, toys thrown, yells and laughter. The Negro woman sat through it all like a scholar in a library. Something wet licked at Honey's sandaled foot.

"*Alors*, go 'way cat. The trouble eez he does not want a wife. He does not want a ba-be. Not really, and I don't blame heem. It ees the kind of man he ees. I ne-vair meet a man who ees loving his freedom so. You know somezing. I can not be cruel, not to heem. I really can not. Go *away* cat. You like my dirty feet, eh? I can't be, how you say, a beetch. Yet I want to help heem. Can you believe it. Val is such a boy. Re-lee. I like that in heem and also the way he ess, you know, in bed."

"You've been living with this joker, how long? Ten days? Twelve days? And then 'cause I can't take care of your baby you move out on him? Child, that's an insult to him. Just movin' out like that. Jesus, don't you see it? Damn it, tell 'im you have a baby. And you French and all. Christ, I thought them French was liberal."

"Ah, no I can not. I don't know why. I really don't."

There was a general outburst again. Laughter and crying. The doorbell. The teakettle, and the alarm clock in Honey's bag.

"Child, why on earth don't you buy a wrist watch or a sundial or something. That damn thing's always scaring the bejaises out of me."

"I will be going now," said Honey, as her friend ran off to attend to four things at once. "Tsh, go 'way, cat."

Supporting a face of gloom, she carried her child to the doorway, and there she stiffened with revulsion.

"Hi," said a big, smiling Irish cop, "would you like to buy two tickets to the Police Athletic Ball?"

The train ride seemed shorter each time. Jacqueline cried once, and then became awestruck and patient again. With the ceiling fan flicking the ends of her hair, Honey rubbed noses with the child, made faces, laughed and started all over again. When she climbed, sweating, out of the grimy subterranean hotbox of the subway into the relatively fresh afternoon air, she realized that the baby, spluttering and kicking, was getting hungry. Soon she would cry.

At her building, the dim tunnel was damp and chilly. She emerged into the small, sky-lit courtyard, approached a door and entered the hallway. Once inside her room, she went to the window to pull down the shade and was just in time to see Val striding across the courtyard. She sat still as the door quivered with pounding. Her great fear was that Jacqueline would cry. She rocked and played with the child as the knocking continued. Until the noise ceased, Honey hated all men everywhere. She peeked through the shade to make sure he was gone, but there he stood, alone in the courtyard, like someone waiting for a bus and looking a bit forlorn. *Jesus, child, tell him about the baby.* For a moment Honey considered running out, kissing him and revealing all. But what if he didn't really want her, didn't want both the baby and her? In not keeping her secrets, how would she keep her womanhood? She would be nothing. After all, one gave away what was worthless and held back the things of value. Then the baby cried aloud, and Honey froze. But Val, who had already taken his one last look at her window, had turned that very moment and left.

Honey fed the baby and put her to sleep. Then she stretched out on the day bed and escaped into sleep herself. When she awoke in darkness hours later, she felt vacant and worthless. Things grew worse with the lights on and the pint of rye she found in the closet was all but dead. Sitting Indian-style on the mattress, she drank what little was left and waited. It made her feel no better, and now all her cigarettes were gone as well. Jacqueline was still asleep when Honey carried her upstairs to the apartment of a Greek family who often took care of the child when she had a modeling appointment.

Her first stop was a bar around the corner where there was a waitress who, if pressed, would usually lend her a few dollars. But, as luck would have it, this was Sally's night off. Next she thought of going to Val for the twenty he kept promising to pay back, yet never did. She decided to put this off, however, for she was unwilling to dilute what feeling he might still have for her by making a demand for money. Then she remembered Buzz and where he worked and how he had often asked her to drop around to see him. A train took her to midtown, an elevator took her to the rooftop restaurant, and there he was in the red jacket behind the bar where he smiled and made her a drink. She sat chatting with him for hours, relating nonstop all the latest happenings in her life. When he generously presented her with a third free drink, she turned down the corners of her mouth to show that she was duly impressed. But it occurred to her that he had a plan afoot, especially when he asked her to sit and wait for him until closing time. Married men who played this game annoyed her, and so she slowly proceeded to break his masculinity. She began by putting forward as the topic of conversation all the men who ever had a place in her life, and with each detailed description of a past love she felt the two of them moving gradually away from each other though they remained motionless on either side of the bar.

He kept offering drinks, watching her talk and growing, she could tell, more angry and mute. She put on her charming, untouchable high school look with its soft sophomoric glow and talked constantly and moved constantly, tapping a cigarette and waiting for his light, rotating her drink, stretching for a pretzel, scratching a knee, smoothing her skirt and pushing a stubborn bra strap out of sight. When she stopped, on those rare occasions, to let him talk, she mocked him with an intent look of seductive innocence.

The cocktail lounge had a religious stillness, an antiseptic readiness, a sense of timeless isolation which calmed her and made her feel much better. She glanced at the faces around her, but none looked interesting except that of an older man, on the other end of the horseshoe bar, who was studying her with his fuss-and-feathers, slightly humorous, firm and fatherly face, looking like what'shisname? Like that Secretary of State under Truman. Then she saw Utah De Lux enter the restaurant end of the room, sit at a table with a young man and wave at Honey without inviting her to join them.

An hour and a half later when Honey left (she had had her fill of pretzels, and the liquor was beginning to take its toll), she realized, as she waited for the elevator to arrive, that she had forgotten to ask Buzz for money and that now, because she had so foolishly annoyed him, it was too late. The ascent of the elevator seemed endless, and a small crowd gathered with her to wait. That older man was among them; the one who looked like what'shisname? Dean Acheson. She was feeling just drunk enough to ask *him* for some money when the elevator arrived, the doors parted and there was Val and she was saved.

"I'm so happy to see you, you have no idea," she almost said, but didn't. They stood pressed together in close quarters as they descended to the street, and she tried to get him to come home with her and failed. His immunity to her charms was exasperating, and though she longed to follow him wherever he went, her solemn promise to reclaim her baby by midnight prevented this. She resolved to let him in on the secret of her child if he would only come home with her. Then, perhaps, she would even have the courage to declare her love for him as well. But he insisted that he had a job to do and his manner, as usual, was carefree and casual, immune and exasperating. She did get the twenty from him but then there was Utah again like a one-eyed longshoreman and, before she knew it, Honey was left in the lobby all alone.

Manhattan Island moved an inch. She regained her balance. Steady in those heels, she told herself. A herd of cars stampeded down Fifth Avenue. From across the street an electric sign scolded her in red letters. DON'T WALK. Honey good girl. Does what she is told. Very discreet. And sort of high. She was now told to WALK, and so she did, wavering just perceptibly. The great white lion resting happily beside his mate was gazing into a display window across the street. Honey walked west. A fire was burning at the bottom of a litter basket producing a charred smell of outdoor childhood; all those lost innocent late afternoons when she was neither a girl nor a boy, just young and running and playing the part of a child. DON'T WALK. She didn't. WALK. She did. Good girl. Manhattan moved again. Whooops.

"Are you all right, Miss?"

A bow tie like a butterfly.

"Are you all right?"

"Y'all so kand to ask."

"Thought you might be ill."

"Ah should always be this ill."

"Can you tell me where the Village is?" he asked.

"What village? What city y'all want?"

Looking puzzled: "I was told … somewhere down …"

Giggling: "Oh, Grain-itch Village."

"You see, I just hit town. Linen buyers convention and all that."

She watched the bow tie wobble as he spoke.

"Say, haven't ah seen y'all before? Wayer?"

"Where?" he smiled.

"Dean Acheson, that's it."

He was puzzled again.

"At the bar wayer ah just came from?"

After a shy series of nods and a movement of his shoe, like a pawing hoof, he admitted all. Back at the cocktail lounge, he had been so smitten that he couldn't keep himself from following her. He tried but he couldn't. Sorry, no offense meant. He was simply all alone in a strange city. Had she ever been lonely?

"You know somethin'," said a beaming Honey Bea. "That taah fascinates me."

The black stripes at his neck wobbled as he said: "Well, thank you." Then, indicating a corner tavern:

"May we?"

"*Mais oui*," she said.

It was nothing like the other place. On the bar stood a tulip row of yellow beers. Everyone was turned, heads up, toward the square of light. Gunshots carried across an empty Western plain, then men on horses galloped, then more shots.

"Ah saw this picture," she said and ordered a beer.

Jack was his name. She told him hers, and the room went into a blurred quarter turn. She promptly made it stop. They moved about through the conversation like two even-tempered badminton players who were new at the game.

"Oh, an actress," said Jack, "how interesting."

Above the gunfire, she told him all about her experiences in Hollywood, and before she knew it her beer was gone and there was a Scotch on the rocks in its place. Don't touch it, she told herself, or you'll get sick. He, on the other hand, was sweating. When she turned to the TV again a commercial was on.

"Take your jacket off if you're hot," she heard herself say, too late, for his jacket was already off, revealing twin vertical stains of shirt sweat.

The room went into another blurred quarter turn. This time as soon as she made it stop it started again. The walls just had to be induced to stand still, and she concentrated her attention toward this end. When the room persisted in pulling and tugging at her reins, she proposed a walk. He proposed a ride. She didn't remember accepting, yet off they rode in a lurching cab with the meter ticking special meaning into each new minute and quarter of a mile. He was explaining something, was good old Jack. But what?

"You bet," she said, with her head back and sucking in oceans of air from the open window.

She threw herself several times against her plywood door until finally it yielded them her furnished room and a half.

The first thing she did was place water on the stove. Then she ran up two flights to retrieve a sleeping Jacqueline and carry her back down to the crib in the tub.

"Yours?" he asked when she came in from the hall.

"Mine," she answered as she marched to the bathroom.

The hissing tongues of the blue flame had not yet disturbed the pot of still water as Honey returned, apologized and asked him to sit down. He remained on his feet and studied the photos on the wall.

"I also like the movies," he said.

"Do y'all thank it's true," she asked, indicating her gallery of stars, "that great beauty brings sadness?"

"I dunno. I never had a great beauty."

She giggled. "Ah mean brings sadness to the one who's beautiful. She tried to kill herself, Brigitte. Cut her wrists and all. Ah was so upset."

Honey glanced at the pot again. It was making sizzling sounds though the water remained still. The onslaught of alcohol was lessening, however, and she rejoiced. The danger had passed.

"I go to the movies a lot," he said, turning away from the wall.

"You know what ah enjoy most?" she said, thinking: why the hell doesn't he sit down? "This'll sound funny to you but ah lak the comin' attractions. Theyar so excitin', don't you think? You don't hayave to bother with a story. You just sort of get the best of everathing."

"Oh, yes, I agree." And he edged closer.

Something's going to happen, *she thought.* I can feel it.

The pot was making more assertive noises. She had been looking for a cigarette, and he opened his silver case like a prayer book, the initials J.F. on the front. Like a practiced magician, he produced a matching cigarette lighter already aflame.

"Ah thankya kindly."

She didn't want to sit on the day bed with him, but there was nowhere else.

"In a minute we'll hayave some coffee," she said, going to the dresser to turn on a table lamp, thinking: *The more light the better.* "Y'all sit down niaeow and I'll..."

She was walking past him on the way to the stove, pausing for a moment beside the stack of magazines on the table (*Motion Picture, Modern Screen, Playboy*), to bend and pick up a cup and saucer standing there from the night before when he reached out and, in an almost fatherly manner, cupped her soft right rump.

She scolded him with a word or two, nothing much, and then she backed away carrying the empty cup on its saucer as though she were about to lift it with trained delicacy to her lips, her frightened face looking mostly bored.

"Well, come on," he said.

"Sit down, niaeow."

He moved in as though for the kill, his bow tie bobbing as he said: "Come on, will ya."

"Please, Mr...." She realized she didn't know his last name. "You'll have to stop this. Please sit!"

"Fowler," he said.

"Mr. Fowler," she repeated.

"Ah don't want to hayave to tell you again," she added.

Reaching out, he took hold (as if it were a doorknob) of her left breast. The cup trembled on its saucer and fell, its little one-eared snake-curl of a handle now missing as it rolled along the linoleum. Pulling free, she held up the small saucer as if it were a shield.

"Come on," he almost shouted. "What's wrong anyway?"

"A'm just going to hayave to ask y'all to leave."

"Oh, you are, are you?"

He unbuckled his belt and again, like a practiced magician, cracked it free of his pants.

The phone rang.

She had retreated to the rear of the living room while he stood with the door on his right and the phone on his left and able to get to either of them before she could. He took a single forward stride. Her face still looked bored. She ordered him to stop, and the phone rang again.

"Come on," he insisted.

The phone rang a third time.

Hanging from his hand, the belt dispersed a light clutter of dust on the living-room floor.

Honey adjusted her tumbling hair as though worried about her looks.

"That's for me," she said.

"Let it ring."

And it did again as though in protest.

"Come *on*, damn it."

"*No*," she answered, equally loudly.

Then his belt cracked loudly, and the saucer dropped and broke. The candle rocked as she backed into the dresser, clutching her thigh.

"*Come*," he whispered menacingly, "*on*."

Her head trembled in a final display of annoyance and capitulation. "*Ou*," she said angrily. Then it was over.

"O.K., Mac, don't make a federal case of it." For a brief moment it was a different Honey with a different voice. "You'll be goddamn sorry, I warn ya."

The period of silence between each cadence of ringing became, at this point, stretched and pulled out of shape until she realized that the phone was done with ringing. Sitting on the day bed, she hiked up her black skirt to unhitch her black stockings, flashing a patch of bleached thigh.

"Why will I be sorry?" he asked.

Her eyes widened. "Because," she said, her tone muted as though they were in a public place where one must struggle with discretion, "because a'm havin' ma *period*."

"Don't tell me *that's* the reason for all this fuss."

He stood with amazement, holding the belt as if it were a dead snake, his trousers slipping a little on his waist, breaking heavily on his shoes. She seemed mute with shame, and she didn't look up until a thought occurred which caused her eyes to leap at his. He made an ostentatious two-handed display of his belt, and she went on with the job of unzipping her skirt. Abused and scuffed, her consciousness went awash with whiskey for a while and the patterns of shame and hatred blended and dissolved.

She crossed her arms and pulled the blouse over her head, her hair standing straight up for a moment.

"Oh, it's false," she said, watching him unclip the bow tie. "Ah thought it was real."

He dropped his shirt and tie on the magazine pile and studied her: "Well, there's nothing false about you, now, is there?"

She, in turn, took time out to inspect her thigh for a possible strap mark. *The dirty rat bastard.* But her anger slipped away despite her efforts to hold it, and it was in this mood that she made love, each man reduced to being nothing more than an accomplice in her plans for self-punishment. Having been naughty with one man, she got back at herself by committing another naughtiness with the next, making it necessary, of course, to continue each naughtiness with a lasting series of retributions. The water on the stove boiled to a crescendo as their bodies wrestled through the same incessant movement like two figures in a trick motion picture sequence. He stood up and with a carpet of thick hair running from neck to groin, went off and returned carrying the towel she had requested, having turned off the water as well. He lifted the heap of sharkskin from the floor and it became a pair of trousers from whose pocket a ten-dollar bill was produced and extended. With a dour face, she was inching away from the dark stain that had spread out on the sheet beneath her. Then she saw the money, and her expression took on a hard, disapproving look.

"Take it," he insisted, in a tone that meant he sensed trouble.

"No."

"Take it."

She shook her head.

He screamed like a woman. "*You little bitch, take it.*"

Nothing at all from her now.

"Why?" he was stunned. "Tell me why?"

She sat straight. "Thyat's the way a girl gets into the business."

"One ten-spot don't make a hooker."

"A girl tries to be good, and just look what it gets her."

"Oh, come off it. Here take this."

"Why give your money away? Save it. A'm goin' to be an actress."

"Sure you are, baby."

"Y'all don't know what hustlin' can do to a girl's lafe."

"If y'all curious," she continued. "Ah'll tell you what it does, ah really will. Y'all get to sleepin' late. You miss all the interviews and tryouts and you never get a chance to model which is a way of gettin' known and perhaps gettin' a small part in somethang. You miss all that and besides you work all night and don't have no social lafe and never get to go to the movies and ah know cause it happened to this friend of mine, it really did."

What he thought was his experienced understanding of the situation had become, from the look on his face, suddenly upended. He scrambled for something on the floor and came up with his belt. The ten-dollar bill, tossed on the bed, was standing on its edge. He commanded her for the last time to take the money. She tried to scramble out of the way but her condition, with the towel between her legs, caused her to flounder. She yelped at the sound more than at the pain, though her thigh was pulsating with a hot cluster of needle stings. He raised the strap again. She made a quick fist; the bill was in it.

"O.K., she said. "O.K., O.K."

"Then you take it?" He was still not sure.

"Y'all must be sick. I mean it. That really hurts."

"Do you take it or not?"

"Why y'all so excitable?"

Up went the strap.

"O.K. Yes. All right. Ah take it. See. Ah take it."

"Holy mackerel," he said, wiping his forehead with his forearm. "You know something? You're the toughest I've ever had. I kid you not."

He got dressed. She sat examining her thigh, leaning on the fist that held the money as though she had forgotten all about it and his presence in the room as well. He watched her awhile; then after an appropriate pause, an appropriate official pause, he said: "O.K., let's go."

She looked up at him, her hand still rubbing her skin.

"Get dressed," he said. "I'm taking you in."

Through the screened window, she could see over the top of the Village where the tarred rooftops stretched out in psychotic disorder. Down below, several streets came together in a pushing tangle of Saturday night activity that resembled a mob scene in a film spectacular. Daylight was slowly deserting her, and as far as she could see the idle world walked whichever way it wished, unaware that she even existed.

A hand slid up her bare leg. Honey jumped away from the window, tripped and fell. The officer, a fat, freckled woman, stared down at her with grinning insolence.

"Where's my baby?" Honey asked, getting up.

"Can't you ever think of nothin' else to say?"

"What's going to happen to my baby?"

The officer made to stroke the blond cheek. "Come here and I'll tell ya."

Honey pulled away.

"Come here and I'll tell you about your baby."

"You have news of my baby?"

"Sure, come here."

"Will they take her away from me?"

"Come here and I'll whisper into your ear."

Honey wanted to punch the walls, to scream out the window and at the same time become a model of good behavior. She wanted to punish the whole world and also become its prize citizen. It was the thought of Jacqueline in someone else's arms, cared for or neglected by a state-appointed stranger that cut to the bone.

They had forced her to undress with the others. They had forced her to shower and climb into prison clothes. She was given a pair of black, badly worn oxfords with Cuban heels, two pairs of socks marred by repeated mendings, three gray cotton dresses, two cotton slips, two pairs of panties and a couple of flat, totally useless bras which she couldn't wear at all. Her request for a better fit was ignored.

Then, standing in the hall, not joining the general conversation, she waited. It was a long wait, and when the doctor arrived he did so on the run, a pack of cigarettes and some pens bulging out of his shirt. No time was wasted, for the doctor seemed driven. Three women, two Negro and one Chinese, were pushed into the doctor's office. Honey, a young Puerto Rican and an old woman of about fifty were the next in line. They waited and then entered together. "Can you help me find out about my baby?" Honey asked, but she was made to strip and climb onto a table while the two others watched, also naked, waiting their turn. A cold speculum was thrust into her. She was wiped with a wet cotton swab. Something else was thrust in. There was an injection of liquid. "There you are," said the doctor, handing her a piece of cotton to mop up with. "Next!"

"About my baby…" The doctor knew nothing about it; Honey was soon out in the hall again feeling slimy and ugly and utterly forsaken.

It seemed a reasonable fear, this belief she had that she would go mad. A narrow toylike cell, the broken-spring bed, the not knowing about Jacqueline, the ceaseless exposure of herself to all of those exposed to her, the slow, unticking timelessness and the listening, whether she wished to or not, to a city of free people doing as they pleased without even the slightest need of her. The sentence was for sixty days. She had come to the point where she just could not go on any more. And she had been in her cell for no longer than fifteen minutes.

"Well, love, what'ch in fer?"

This was her cell mate from the other side of the world.

Honey, in the act of praying, lifted her head as though she had been slapped on the back.

"Please, you wheel be so kind as to forgive my 'orrible accent."

"Hey, you Spanish or somethin'?"

"Iyam from Fronce. Iyam born in Paris."

"Crazy. What they get you on?"

"Smuggling ze jewelry of my lovair."

"No kidding? Nooooo kidding? Crazy."

Later, when her cell mate was asleep and snoring, Honey lowered her head again and prayed. "Please God, I don't like this place. God, take me out of this place. Please. I really mean it. Make them give Jacqueline back. Don't let them keep her forever. Please don't let them do that. From now on I'll go to bed early and I'll clean my room and I'll study. I'll study so I won't be stupid any more. I promise. And I'll be good, very good. I won't go to bed with anyone until at least the third date, God, I promise. I really do. And make them give me my child back. She's my child, not theirs. Make them, God. You can do it if you really want. Come on, God. Be good to me. I need someone to be good to me. I never had anyone. I really never did."

If you don't sleep near the wall, the spring gets you right in the back. Oh, I wish her snoring would stop. Fagged-out old slut. She scares me but I mustn't be frightened. I mustn't go crazy. Then they'll never give her back to me. Oh, that son of a bitch judge with his red freckled face. Sitting up there like nothing in the whole world could touch him. Just listening. Q: Officer, did you arrest the defendant in this case at twelve thirty A.M. at 164½ Sixteenth Street? A: I did. Q: Will you tell the circumstances that prompted you to make this arrest? A: I met the defendant about eleven thirty on the southeast corner of Sixth Avenue and Thirty-eighth Street. She smiled and said hello to me. I said I was in the city with a linen convention. She said, do you want to have a good time for ten dollars? I said, sure but what do I get for that? She said, whatever you want. I said, do you french? and she said, not usually but for you I'll make an exception. We went to her home. She stripped down to just her bra and said I want my money first. Then I arrested her. Q: When did you discover she had a baby in the back room? A: At just about that time. *That filthy liar!* Why do men lie to hurt others? Dirty rat bastard. Why did he do that? "I'm not a hustler," I said. "What happened to your accent?" he asked. Screaming: *"I'm not a hustler. You forced me, you bastard. You beat me."* "Come on, get dressed," he said, standing there all tired and official-looking, dull and flat-sounding, snapping his tie back on. *"You slept with me. You're a cop. I hate cops. You're scum. You're SCUM."* He said: "Can it, lady. I've had a hard day. Get dressed. Get the kid. And let's go." I took the towel from between my legs—it was heavy with blood—and I threw it.

Darkness has no walls or ceiling. You can hear buses on Sixth Avenue. Never thought you could be so close to The Figaro, to Julius' and still be in jail. Damn rotten bed. And that snoring. Her stuff lying all around. Toilet water, the jar of sour balls, a half-eaten Milky Way. And never offering any. Her face like a long-haired Burt Lancaster. Can hear the leftover fireworks from the Fourth of July. Small room. Mustn't go crazy. Oh, for a movie. I'll miss *Irma La Douce*, maybe, and *Hud*. Sixty days is a long time. All those picture shows I'll miss. The going inside and feeling the air conditioning grip you. And that smell which is no smell at all. The clear, air-conditioned nonsmell of the picture show. Quiet carpets. Coke machines. Candy stands. All hushed and in their place, and you can hear the mumbled speech from the screen before you are even inside where you can sit and be no one and take off your shoes and laugh when you hear a man drop all his change out of his pocket on the dark floor and listen to it roll away and watch the lovers neck and count their kisses and, if you're lucky, see the coming attractions twice. But then there's the pain of coming out again, back into the baked, exhausted afternoon. Walking not like myself but like the heroine, Audrey Hepburn or Marilyn Monroe, talking like her, thinking like her, actually being her, the certainty of being someone else.

"Come here and I'll tell ya."

"No."

"Come here and I'll tell you about your baby."

"You have news of my baby?"

"Sure, come here."

"Will they take her away from me?"

"Come here and I'll whisper into your ear."

"All right. What? What is it? Tsh, stop. Don't. Stop it. Let me go."

"O.K., I'll tell you what. Now I *will* tell ya. You ain't going to see that baby, no more, ever. That's what."

"A lie."

"They goin' to put it in a home what gives babies away to people. But I can help you if ya friendly. If ya ..."

"No. A lie."

"They goin' to put it in this home what gives babies away to strangers, and your baby will love these strangers and call dem Mommie and Daddy, that's what, and she'll not even know you at all. Do you like that? Do you? Hey. Stop screaming, you idiot. Listen to me. Come back here."

The corridor was crowded with cotton gray forms awaiting nine o'clock and lights out. The bulbs in the ceiling, guarded with scrotum-shaped mesh, cast a contorted design of yellow and gray across the faces and hands of all those who turned and saw "Frenchy" running hysterically from the direction of the last cell, like someone putting the last burst into a fifty-yard dash, only to collide with a woman standing as fixed as a tree and bounce away into a cluster of forms where she lay, in the middle of the mayhem that followed, pounding the floor and screaming for her child and God.

Freedom proved to be as much a prison as the one they had kept her in for eight weeks. On the morning of her release, she went directly to a movie house on Forty-second Street and before the day was up she had spent more than twelve hours in four theaters and would have done the same the following day but her money dwindled down.

She phoned Val for help, and a Miss Francheska Luca answered and said it was all right for Honey to appear the next evening and go to work. On her way uptown, Honey cautioned herself against tears and carefully rehearsed the story of how she had been away in California doing film work. In the studio, the July humidity and the hot lights baked her body so that the sweat poured from her without stopping, and though a dozen men crowded the room with their own heat and silence, peering at her through their cameras, she was much comforted by Val's presence, realizing for the first time how much she had missed him.

But that part of her recent past which she was trying to bury and forget leaped up at her again when Val, after they were alone, mentioned quite pointedly that he had seen her on the street with a little baby in her arms. She tried at first to avoid the subject and then deny it, but he kept hammering home the fact that the baby he saw was hers until at last she felt herself torn apart with rage and tears. She stood firm, however, and disclaimed her own mother-hood. It was too humiliating to do otherwise.

Though she returned several times to the studio to pose, it took a full week or more before she could fully trust herself alone with Val again to play the part of Honey Bea without worrying about breaking down. It was on a Saturday evening when her confidence fully returned. She was sitting at a bar with a young man (one of a lustful team of three; by name: Knox, Cox and Fox) when who should stroll by trying to find his abandoned beer on the crowded bar, grinning to himself about some comic fluke of life, but the one man in this world she most wanted to see.

INTERVIEW

HONEY Bea, model and starlet, lives in a one-room, rear-building, ground-floor apartment on West Sixteenth Street where the only place to sit (a black canvas contour chair has been torn beyond use) is an overstuffed day bed with brown animals gaily dancing on a background of bright yellow. Above the bed, taped to the wall, is a studio glossy of Elizabeth Taylor between one of Eddie Fisher and another of Richard Burton. There is also a newspaper photo of Montgomery Clift with reverse print showing through from the other side. A few inches away, the docile waters of the Mediterranean are gently bathing the piquant curves of Brigitte Bardot as she lies face down, naked and smiling, on the sands of the Riviera.

Between a small green lamp and a wax-covered wine bottle, there stands on the dresser a torn and shabby lineup of paperback editions of Peyton Place, Anatomy of a Murder, Marjorie Morningstar, The Carpetbaggers *and* The American Tragedy.

A towel hanging from the knob keeps the bathroom door stuck shut. Somewhere a large clock is heard ticking. In the middle of an empty coffee table is an ashtray filled with bobby pins. The rest of the barely furnished apartment reveals about as much of her personality as would a hotel room rented for the night.

Wearing what she calls "my new snug summer dress," Miss Honey Bea gives the appearance of a well-packaged delivery of ripe fruits and melons. Her age is deceiving. She looks sixteen at one moment and almost thirty the next. In conversation, she jabs and tugs at the interviewer to stress a point, slaps his knee in gay reproach and above all else abstains from silence.

HONEY: What kind of personality do you want? Sweet? Sexy? What?

INTERVIEWER: Whichever you wish. I hate to say it, but why don't you just be yourself?

HONEY: Oh, God, what a thought. No, let me see. I'll be ... I know. O.K. Go on. Ask me questions. I'm ready.

INTERVIEWER: You look very happy today. Any special reason for this?

HONEY: It's a discovery I've made. I'm married four months, I have a twelve-month-old baby and guess what? I find I'm in love with my husband. I really am. I love four things: the movies, my family, acting and screwing. Oh, listen to me, I'm awful. My life always seems to be happening the wrong way around. Most people leave their parents and go out on their own. But my parents left me. They went to Europe and so there I was on my own at fourteen. Say, when did *you* first lose your virginity?

INTERVIEWER: Since this is for publication, I think we should be a little more ...

HONEY: Oh, to hell with that. You can cut out the parts you don't like. Come on, when did you lose your virginity? From the looks of you it was maybe a month after you got married. Nasty, huh? O.K., I lost mine at twelve. That was nothing. I almost lost it at nine when I tried to seduce my little brother.

INTERVIEWER: You have a brother? Your agent didn't mention this or that you had a family either.

HONEY: I have one brother, now dead, who I love and a sister in Jersey who I hate. She's one of those goodie-goodies living in a ranch home with her two and a half children and her potential ten-thousand-dollar-a-year husband. They have stereo with hundreds of records and not one piece of dance music. I mean it. Can you beat that? But I'm not jealous of her. I was in love five times and married twice.

INTERVIEWER: You were married twice? Your agent didn't say anything about that either.

HONEY: Yes, I was married twice. My first husband, he was a
real lousy bastard. I lived with my second husband
for seven months—he's away now in prison—and
we must have set some kind of record for screwing.
Twice a day for a year. It's tiring. But more so for a
man. A woman can fake it, but a man can't. I love
my mother, really. When I got pregnant everybody
kept telling me to get married. I was this big but I
was stubborn. Finally, I got married. When I got my
first abortion my mother was nice enough to pay for
it. She's a doll. But I can't take her for long. I can't
take anyone for too long. Yes, even my husband. I
don't know how we lived together as long as we did.
It must have been hell. I guess it was. I do whatever
I want to do. I live for now, for my career, my modeling, and going to the movies. I love my husband,
but how long can it last? Four years? Five years? Six
at most. So I live now and I don't let anyone stop
me. You know, when I had my baby I had it home, I
really did. No hospital for me. You know what they
do to babies? They circumcise them. Can't imagine
jumping on a little baby and cutting off a piece of its
flesh. Part of its penis. It's criminal. It's savage. I had
my baby home and I had to do most of the work. My
husband was my doctor's assistant. That's when he
first began to go insane. Watching me have a baby.
It was too much for him. He's in a mental hospital
now and comes home on weekends. You know how it
was when I first had my baby? Four hours later I had
to go out looking for a job. It was awful. I had no
money for subway fare so I took a cab. But I love my
husband. I have never committed adultery. It's just
that we were always so poor. So I did modeling for

a living. An artist's model at first and then photography work. I have a voluptuous body. Do you think I have a good body? I do. *(Taking off one of her shoes.)* And look at that arch. As good as Pavlova. I used to dance, too. You should see my figure, it's great. You look indifferent, you bastard. I bet you're married. You know what I love to do? I love to go to parties with my husband, take him into the bathroom and make love with him in the bathtub. With the door locked, of course. I once sold my body for a hundred dollars. To an old man. It was nothing. He knew everything. He was, you know, a virtuoso. But nothing from the heart. He said, it won't do you much harm and it will do me a lot of good. I liked that. And it was wonderful spending the money. People are just afraid to live. They're ugly inside and out. There should be more fucking, that's what. I have sixty-five maybe seventy years left and the thing is to live. I'm eighteen and if the next eighteen are as good as the last, wow, I should have a ball. I want to have more babies and I want to go back to school. I want to become a movie star and make a great film with Fellini. I love him, I really do. I love four things. The movies, acting, my family and screwing. In fact, I'm acting right now. I'm always acting, I really am. Do you want a can of beer, by the way? Look at me, I'm doing so much talking I figure *your* throat is dry. Well, what other questions do you want to ask me? I've seen every film Gregory Peck ever made. I can list them. You want to hear? I didn't think so. His films are about basic human emotions. About man's love for mankind. He and Alan Ladd I love best. They're my favorite actors. And I love Montgomery Clift, too. And Liz Taylor, she slays me. Boy would I love to live her kind of life, I really would. I'm not kidding. Someday I will. In a way I guess I'm doing it already. Bardot, I'm not so sure. I think she's much too wild. I heard some of the things she's done. I really mean it, I think you can go too far.

SHE CAME down into the street where a crowd of men stood waiting to look her over. Since she had already been hired, and there was no turning back, the inspection was all the more severe. She stopped to examine the mocha-cream sky to prolong the capture of everyone's attention, for she imagined herself surrounded by worshipers, each desperate to acquire her signature on a scrap of paper. Then she turned to one of the men in the same way a movie star might chat with a stagehand. "If it rains," she said, "I'll never trust the *Daily News* again. I really won't."

Twenty men in all stood on the sidewalk studying the sky, the blonde and one another. There was a noiseless, closed-for-the-day appearance to the street, though Broadway was at one end and Sixth Avenue at the other. On the roof opposite stood a mushroom growth of black chimneys. Below was the window of an employment agency, below that the imperfect lettering of an UP OLSTERY CORP, and on the street level was a diamond dealer whose gates were closed and locked.

The door through which Honey appeared swung open again and Val, knotting his tie, came forth grinning. He had a quick step and a playfulness of spirit that conflicted with all the dreary morning faces and the general pessimism about the weather.

"Anyone for a monsoon?" he quipped, to no one's great pleasure, and his emaciated frame quivered with mute laughter. With tousled hair, he looked volatile, alert and underfed. He made the tie, cinched it to his neck, found the narrow end longer than the other and started all over again.

Honey stepped up and pertly placed herself face to face with him, pointing to the sky in a pretended mope of dismay. Though she wished him to stay and chat, he tweaked her nose and turned to answer questions thrown at him by his worried customers. Yes, they would get their money back if it rained. Yes, there was a second girl coming. No, he didn't sell film. Yes, they would all be back by six.

Val finished making his tie again. This time, however, it hung too long, and he sighed and began once more. Carrying her feed-bag pocketbook, Honey left him, wriggled four fingers and ducked into the Mercury where she sat with the slanted image of a print shop down the street double-exposed upon her face. Val wriggled back, imitating her delicate impishness. Then, resuming with his tie, he called for three volunteers to drive the three other cars parked along the curb. At last giving the signal for everyone to climb aboard, he bounced in beside the blonde.

"Are we all snug and comfy?" he asked, his mannered enthusiasm implying a private joke. With his face almost grotesquely narrow and with his fingers still working at his throat, he glanced at those in the rear.

"The boxed lunches," Honey cried, touching his knee.

"Christ." And Val bounced from the car into the building.

After inspecting her hair in the rearview mirror, there still remained a few moments to wait. A young woman led a tottering child across the street and Honey, suddenly noticing them, shut her eyes. Grief had recently burst in on her and, for a while, it had been a struggle just to keep her balance. To save herself, she would sometimes playact the role of the grieving mother, borrowing synthetic feelings to cover up and stifle her true ones. Or, imitating an actress, maintain a flow of gaiety which enabled her even better to endure the loss of her child. But, occasionally, when caught off guard, such theatrics failed her, and once again she bled, remembering her loss. She had been out of prison for only three days, and the sight of the empty crib was painful enough, not to mention that first night after they set her free when Val kept questioning her about Jacqueline and she kept denying everything until all at once she was sobbing while floodlights pinned her to the wall. These memories (the hollow of the crib, Val's probing, a woman walking with her child) she now erased from her mind until once again she was innocent of grief, ingenuous and cheerful, and devoid of a past.

Cramped into the cars and still half asleep, the twenty men and one young woman sat and waited. From the moment he climbed into the back seat, Victor Ottomeyer found himself making concessions to a copper-haired, crew-cut, boldly broad-shouldered man on whose face was pinned one of those all-purpose half-smiles of the always cheerful. To the right of this man sat a meager, molelike gentleman who needed a shave and wore a wild Hawaiian shirt.

The blonde up front was something to see. Snuggled in between the resolute man in the peaked cap and that crazy one called Val, she was, Ottomeyer felt, one of those females who can contribute much without talking at all. Her expression, when anyone spoke to her, appeared to be saying: "See how hard I am listening, how much I am learning. Oh, do keep talking." Then, usually, there followed that incidental nodsmile of hers which wholeheartedly endorsed nothing. Also eloquent in silence were her bold breasts augmented by her black sleeveless sweater.

It took two trips in and out of the building with his thin, energetic legs moving swiftly beneath a tall stack of boxes before the food was finally all stashed away in the luggage compartment of the Mercury. Once more behind the wheel, Val knotted the tie for the third time, and again the narrow end hung longer than the other, tell-tale and goopy. He reached into Honey's feedbag, touching tissues, a lipstick, two cigarette packs, some loose pages of an address book, a spoon, her plastic diaphragm case, his broken pipe stem, a large, round alarm clock, a paperback *Life of Frank Sinatra* and other things that he couldn't identify. At last finding what it wanted, his hand emerged holding a long pair of scissors with which he made one mighty final snip and threw the offending piece of tie out the window.

As Honey gave a startled little laugh, the broad-shouldered man in back decided that this driver had to be, could be nothing else but, a queer.

Now they were ready. At nine ten the motors started up, except for the Mercury, which was giving Val trouble. The grinding rhythm of engine failure made him shake his head. "This goddamn beat-up wreck. I swear they'll *bury* me in it some day."

The Mercury caught. Val yelled hallelujah, the procession began to move, and then they noticed it.

"Oh, dear," said Ottomeyer.

"Called on account of rain," announced the broad-shouldered man.

"Never any luck," said Val. "Never."

The windshield wipers went to work on the lead car, the left spanning the glass in erratic jumps, the right moving and leaving streaks. The procession motored uptown through vacated streets, halting at a red, resuming at a green, keeping in single file as though going to a funeral.

The rain increased, yet the procession showed no signs of stopping. It hissed over water-slick streets, past dead electric signs and slowed down on Seventh Avenue for an old man who walked as though waterproofed. While yellow cabs pulled up to a length of dry walk at the Coliseum, the procession curved carefully through Columbus Circle and came out onto a rain-glossy, tree-topped Central Park West. As they moved uptown, Val didn't seem bothered by anything, least of all the weather, and he hummed part of a Clementi sonata he had heard that morning on the radio and fingered the wheel as though it were a keyboard.

Ottomeyer snapped at him. "Would you please lift your window, Mr ...." He faltered at the name.

"Valentine Manuel Crotch," said the driver to the accompaniment of Honey's laughter.

"De Franco," said Ottomeyer, remembering it now, quite annoyed. "It's raining in on me."

"Val's the name, charm's the game," said the man with the shoulders who thought the driver was queer.

"My, you *do* have a way with words," said Val quickly.

"Yes, let's tell our names. Don't you think? I'm Honey Bea."

The man with the shoulders said, "Joe Jones here. People call me Jonesy."

Honey swiveled around to receive the introductions with a hostess' indiscriminate smile.

"Nat DeVore," said the peak-capped, corpulent man beside her.

The man in the beard mumbled, "Victor," just to be done with it.

"Harry," announced the man with HARRY stitched on his Hawaiian shirt.

Nat looked deep into Central Park where nothing moved and all was wet and quiet. "Is there any point in going on?" he demanded. "This damn rain, Jesus."

Val shifted into second with difficulty as they pulled away from the intersection. "Hell, this could be the second coming of the Old Testament," he said. "You wouldn't want to miss that, would you?"

"If the rain continues," said the disquieted Nat DeVore, "we'll be throwing away our time and your money."

"We sure as hell will be," Val said.

Such perverse agreement was extremely annoying to Nat, who noticed that none of the others had taken up his cry to turn back. Jonesy explained that his only worry was that the Yankee game would be rained out. Harry said nothing. Val kept humming. Honey yawned her head back onto the seat, looked at the driver and asked: "Aren't you worried? This rain and all. I'd be worried stiff."

"Don't know how to worry," Val answered. "It's my tragic flaw."

The rain struck in an angry torrent, and he hurried the wipers, hoping the damn things would keep working. Otto-meyer groaned at the innundation, whereas Nat DeVore felt vindication and contentment.

"Here it comes," Val announced angrily. "Pour, you bastards, pour."

Thunder split the air above them.

"Tsh," said Ottomeyer, hugging himself as though chilled.

"Boy, look at it pelt the windshield," Jonesy said.

Val glanced into the rearview mirror to see whether the other cars were following. The blurred glass, front and back, crawled with rain. It was so bad that wipers were of no use at all, and as they did their futile, synchronized dance, the talking stopped in order not to interfere with the driver's concentration. It was at that very moment that Val's shoulders began to shake again. The worse things grew the more amused he became.

"Ever see such a downpour?" Honey asked no one in particular. "Aren't you glad you're not out there?"

"They ain't going to play ball today," said Jonesy, while Nat brushed away the nasty rain that had leaked onto his sleeve from the window.

"I remember in Yucatan once it rained like this," said Val. "The road turned to mud as we drove. We finally sank right into it and couldn't move."

They continued in silence until Ottomeyer said nervously: "He can't see what he's doing. Yet he doesn't stop."

"Well," Val smiled, "isn't that the American way?"

"This isn't a joke."

"Red light," warned DeVore, softly, peering like a catatonic at the wind-lashed crossing.

They came to a halt beside a yellow cab where two unidentifiable shapes blurred by the rain were huddled in the rear. Behind and still with them stood the three other cars.

"I always become tired when it rains," said Honey, yawning.

After a few more blocks the downpour softened. Harry pressed his brow against the stained window and glancing up at one of the small, poorly placed New York street signs saw or thought he saw the number "76" fly past overhead. His breath left a blot on the glass. Leaning back wearily, he enclosed himself in a blissful private thought or two concerning the blonde, when Jonesy gave him an elbow in the ribs.

"Ever been out on one of these things before?"

"Never," Harry replied, looking at the window to discourage talk.

Jonesy pressed closer, breathing into his ear. "A real good-lookin' head, this one we're going to pick up. A gasser. Her picture was on the wall back there. You see it?"

Harry retained an unyielding face, trying to cloak interest with dignity.

"She's like the grunt in the mombo," said Jonesy.

Harry's head wobbled a few nods.

"I forget her name. Man, she's a third called strike with the bases filled. Know what I mean?" Harry got the elbow again.

"Well, I'll be damned," Val exclaimed. The blonde's head was firmly on Nat's shoulder, her face neutral in the open-mouthed inertness of sleep.

"Out cold?" Jonesy wanted to know. "How about that?"

"If she's too heavy for you I can wake her," Val said.

"Not at all," Nat DeVore replied. "Let her rest."

"Must have been a hard night," said Jonesy, nudging Harry without looking at him.

Val forced an oncoming Mercedes-Benz to slow up and surrender the right of way as he turned west and led the procession down a side street of brownstones and parked cars. A black and white fox terrier sat in an open window and ceased sniffing to watch them pass. They stopped at Columbus, then made the light at Amsterdam, turning north again when they came to Broadway. Several minutes later the four cars pulled to a stop, the Buick scraping its tires along the curb.

No one really knew what to do next. From several blocks away a tiny bubble of noise began to swell in the midst of the general hubbub of light traffic sounds growing quickly into a wail of anguish and alarm. The siren coming at them from an unknown direction climbed the air with a shriek that was like the touch of an electric current. When it became so loud that it seemed to invert into no sound at all, a police car, its roof bulb flashing, screamed past from behind. At once the air became weighty with a silence that was like a vague disappointment.

Honey awoke at the commotion.

"Was I on your shoulder? Gosh, I'm sorry."

"Quite permissible," Said DeVore.

"You'd think we were old friends or somethin', the way I've been carryin' on."

"I assure you, young lady. It was entirely my pleasure."

"Why, how gallant. You really are."

She leaned forward to see up along the cliff of the building. "What are we doin' here?"

When Val turned the key, the engine ceased with one last tremor. The building seemed to lean forward, threatening him. Inside somewhere, concealed from the world, she had secretly spent the night. He didn't feel jealousy, just a sense of deep disenchantment.

"Are we picking up somebody?" Honey asked, adjusting the rearview mirror to catch sight of her face. "Who are we picking up? Is it Utah?"

"She canceled. This one you don't know."

"Not Miss What'shername? Francheska?"

"No, her name is Tanya." Val opened the door.

"Tanya Lando?" She kept him from leaving the car. "Really? I never worked with her before. I didn't know she did this sort of thing."

"She doesn't. Just like you don't either."

"Oh, another one of those girls who has to eat three times a day."

Val stepped out, closed the door and looked in through the open window. "I leave her in your care, gentlemen. Defend your-selves as best you can."

He trotted away and came right back. "Anyone for cigarettes, Bromo-Seltzer, Band-Aids? Your last chance."

He pointed. Adjacent to the apartment entrance were stacks of Sunday papers piled high on a wooden stand beneath a green awning. The rain tapped him on the shoulder and he went back to work by trotting into the building. 5C, 5C, 5C. Here it is, and he pressed the button, looking at the name. *D. Morganstern.* Was it Digby? Dwight? Derek? Yesterday she had said to him on the phone: "Pressa da five-a-see. I come-ah right down." He moved into the lobby where a man in a torn sweatshirt with a face of solidified hatred was mopping the floor as though forced to by blackmail. Columns. Gothic benches. Deep armchairs chained to the wall. He approached a mirror. A narrow-faced, slim-bodied clown stepped forward. He saw his own head of scrambled hair and his gray summer suit that hung as though still on a hanger. He straightened his tie, swept his hair from his eyes and examined himself. His sad, thin face stared at the hollows of his sad, thin face. He adjusted his posture. Saluted. Struck a casual pose, hand in pocket. Changed it to both hands on his lapels plus a slight slump. Stood straight again. Studied himself some more and then shrugged. "Well, it'll just have to do." He noticed the janitor watching and shot him down twice quickly with first finger and thumb. Then Val slumped into an armchair and checked his watch. Dudley? DeWitt? Dexter? He liked Dexter. Dexter Morganstern. Surely a shit-heel at best. Val lit a cigarette, stretched his legs and waited for the arrow above the elevator to move.

The arrow fell. It stopped at the fifth floor, then continued its descent. The doors pulled open to reveal a stunning young woman calmly seated and applying lipstick with the aid of the elevator mirror. Uncrossing her legs, she got up from the bench and hammered forth with a quick nervous stride which slackened as soon as she spotted him. She shook her head roguishly as though exasperated with all of life itself and as he rose, angry that she was late, he received her perfume all at once. She offered her apologies, her smile and the lovely hollows of her Latin face. He remembered the taste of her long body, the feel of her nipples, and his muscles twitched in blind recognition. Still in evening clothes, she was decked out for the war games of New York night life, and his anger hobbled back with his jealousy in tow.

"Dexter?" he asked, folding his arms.

"What?"

"Or Dudley?"

"Who?"

"D. Morgenstern. Or is it DeWitt?"

"Val, you're looking marvelous. Really. It's wonderful to see you again."

Across the lobby, the handle of the pail rang out as it fell, and Tanya noticed the man in the sweatshirt, his eyes measuring her as though with a tape. The sweep of the mop moved closer, the angry face attentive to her legs instead of his work.

"Oh, let's go," she whispered in disgust, and her high heels hammered the stone floor and down the long archway toward the autos in the rain.

"Comrade," she said, stopping while still on dry ground, "you have American zigarette, no?"

"Don't you *ever* carry your own?" He surrendered a Kent with grumbling reluctance.

"Ve are driving, Comrade, in all dis rain? Ah, by stupid look on face I dink yes, ve are driving in all dis rain." She bent to reach the flame he was shielding in his cupped hands. "De great General Santa-Anna say, sometimes even when everything, she is planned wrong, ve vin."

"Shut up and wait in the car," he said, smiling.

"Which one?"

"I think there's room there in the Buick."

"*You think?* You mean you didn't save a place for me in yours? I've got to sit with a bunch of strangers?" Now all her playfulness was gone, and she pawed her lustrous hair with dramatic displeasure. "You will just never change. *Never, never.*"

"That's what you get for spending the night with a strange man."

"Balls. That's what I get for having anything to do with you."

Several members of the procession, making use of their last chance to buy cigarettes, had run from the cars to the store through the gantlet of rain. Inside was a row of empty phone booths, each with a glass window on the street. The last had two windows, the second looking out on the entrance of the building as well. Into this booth hurried one of the men, rolling the door shut. The others were a safe distance away at the cigarette counter or the magazine rack. Without bothering to sit down, he slapped a number of coins on the shelf below the black phone box and, using a dime from this collection, dialed the operator.

"This is a police call. I want the District Attorney's Office in Catskill County. Person to person to Assistant District Attorney Giles Keith." He recited the number.

Waiting, he glanced at the automobiles standing in the rain, and then with the phone to his ear, he gave an awkward twist to his body so he could inspect, for the second time, the inside of the store. Turning back again he was disturbed by the sight of a beauty standing on the opposite side of the glass that faced the apartment arch. She was one of those women whose excess of sensuality interrupts your thoughts as she passes in the street, exciting the senses and leaving you slightly shaken. Pausing under the arch, she stood face to face with the rain, squinting her displeasure. She received a cigarette and had it lit for her and continued talking. His eyes centered on the outline of her rump and then, hurriedly, he turned away and pronounced his name.

"Got to make this fast…No, they're picking up someone. It's raining like hell down here…You can say that again…Ya. Don't know what they'll do…Check, they're heading for the Willis farm. That much I know…"

Her guarded, curious glance fell on him through the phone booth window as she lifted a newspaper over her head to begin a jolting, high-heeled run through the shower. Val followed, and the door to the Buick opened as they approached.

"There's one babe, wow. Wait'll they drive her ass up there. You'll see. Real cruel. Look, I've got to scoot. What?…"

Tanya waited a moment on the sidewalk holding the paper in the air. She bent forward, her dress going tight and suggestive along the high line of her leg as she stepped from curb to car. Val left her to run back to the Mercury. A couple of men were hurrying from the store.

"Yeh, only twenty in all…The rain, I guess. And the fee's ten dollars. That's two hundred right there. Hey, got to run. Take care. Be good."

He rammed the phone back on the hook, rattled open the door and in a moment was dashing, in a crouch, for the curb. A few seconds later a serene old lady in a transparent raincoat and rain shoes occupied the same booth and said, "Oh, my gracious," when she saw the quarter and three dimes that had been left behind. She turned to report it to someone, but behind her through the glass the curb was already vacant.

AN ECCENTRIC fence followed the procession for a time before taking a drastic right-angle turn and spurting off into the woods. The world became darker briefly as though a huge bird of prey was passing low overhead. Soon it happened again as the gray underbelly of another bridge pressed down and then released them.

The lead car halted under the arch of a toll station. Val's thumb flipped a washer into the Exact Change Basket, a red light turned green and they moved on. The second car chose a different lane and stopped beside an attendant standing in the doorway. Tanya rolled down her window and extended an elegant arm to unpinch a quarter into his waiting hand. She received a dime in return and found herself the subject of that familiar, stop-everything-and-grab-a-quick-look scrutiny. She responded by distorting her face into a puff-cheeked, mash-lipped absurdity, flickering a beserk series of flirtatious winks at him as the Buick carried her away.

The four automobiles proceeded in single file again, the eight windshield wipers still moving like metronomes as sixteen tires spun out a hissing sound on the wet pavement. Val's battered Mercury launched ahead; the Buick followed, accelerating steadily, while the Ford and Studebaker trailed behind.

Joe Jones now observed Nat DeVore who was sitting in front: the camera nut equipped like a pack camel and, with his peaked cap, looking as incongruous as a third-base coach on a hitless team. Harry, in his monogrammed Hawaiian shirt, was equally overequipped. The bearded Ottomeyer, however, with only an Argus in his lap, looked like Mephistopheles with a mother problem.

"Quite a day for a field trip," said Harry by way of polite sarcasm.

"Quite a day for a ball game," replied Jonesy.

A Volkswagen edged alongside. The driver peered straight ahead in a look of open-mouthed horror. Then he violently sneezed himself into a bowing movement that left him sitting more erect than before.

"What film are you using?" Harry asked.

"Film?" said Jonesy, "I don't even know what *camera* I'm using." Then, with a little lying smile: "I'm here on doctor's orders."

"Oh, I see," Harry replied, timid and gullible in the presence of illness.

All at once, fresh country air cleansed his face and he discovered that DeVore, seated directly in front of him, had lowered the window to eject something which the wind, instead, swept back and lodged between Harry's lips. He said nothing, spit air and flung the offending object (a strand of blond hair) away in disgust. It drifted upon pale currents of tobacco smoke only to return, like a weightless touch of fate, to the corduroy ridges of DeVore's brown shoulder.

"May I turn on the radio?" asked Honey, the sweet, innocent, ingenuous Honey whom she was obliged to keep alive as long as Val was seated beside her.

He emerged from deep thought. "The radio? Sure thing."

"You don't need your wipers," Nat suggested. "The rain has ended."

"Why, so it has. Will wonders never cease?"

Honey turned the knob and waited, scanning the moving scenery, thinking how nice it would be to run downhill through all that sea of wheat and maybe fall without caring and roll and never stop. Reaching up, she gently touched Val's hair until she had moved it out of his eyes. She offered him a fluid look of endearment which gained her nothing and she thought: he doesn't love me either, just like all the others. For a moment he pinched and tugged at her chin. She turned on her sad Ingrid Bergman grin but it, too, was wasted. Something was on his mind. Something was wrong.

"The speed limit," Nat warned, "is forty-five."

"I know. It's just no challenge."

"Challenge?"

"To break," Val added, with bogus disappointment.

"Oh, I see." Nat stared straight on. "Speed limits are to be broken."

"Hey, this radio doesn't work," Honey said. "It really doesn't."

Val agreed.

"But you said I could turn it on."

"I said you could turn it on. I didn't say it would work."

She hit him with her featherweight fist. This brought forth his nasal laugh which Honey followed with an imitation Doris Day look of total chagrin.

"Hey, you're going to lose them," she cried, for after weaving in and out of traffic their car had broken into the clear.

"I'm a modern-day Moses leading my people to the Promised Land," Val said, gripping the wheel near the top. "But I want to beat them and get a parking spot."

Honey giggled, then looked to her right to share the joke. But Nat DeVore was absorbed with the dials and lenses of his Rollei. In his peaked-cap corpulence he looked to her like a young Edward G. Robinson miscast in the lead of *The Leo Durocher Story*. Joe Jones, on the other hand, when she glanced into the back was ogling her with a fixed look of hunger to which she beamed back a message of stubborn innocence. In the movies he would play an ex-football hero unable to adjust to private life. How was he in bed? Wam-bam and on the lamb. Just the type.

Of the network of droplets quivering in the center of the windshield more and more broke free, driven by the wind.

"You're doing sixty, young man," Nat remarked.

"Tsh, that's terrible," said Ottomeyer, still facing the glass, his breath clouding it.

"Might get a ticket," Nat warned him.

Patting Honey on the knee: "Tell 'em about me and tickets."

Obediently, she said: "Concerning tickets, sir, well, he tears 'em up."

"I see, he tears them up," said Nat. "How many have you destroyed so far?"

Blowing his horn at a peacefully plodding station wagon: "Don't know exactly. Dozens."

"Dozens. I see."

"Really," said Honey, "he has no regard for anything of—how do you say?—of a legal nature. He's just terrible."

She was so obviously pleased with this aspect of her lover that DeVore could only stare at her and at the driver with amazement.

"You'll be apprehended sooner or later," he predicted. "They're bearing down on scofflaws. Many are getting their licenses revoked."

"Now this they can't do to me."

"Indeed?"

Honey explained: "You see, he hasn't got a license." And she squeezed Val's arm by way of reward. "He's terrible, he really is."

"You haven't got a license?"

"I had one once, years ago. But it expired and I figured, fuck it."

"Oh, I see. That's what you figured." DeVore nodded at the windshield. "You figured that."

"Politzi," Honey warned with vehemence.

The Mercury cut speed and all inside stared in a kind of hushed alliance at a state trooper's parked car.

"I hate police," she snorted, once they were free and clear. She reached for a *cigarette* and at the same time pressed in the lighter on the dashboard.

"Why is that?" Nat asked.

"I just do. All of them."

"You can't be serious."

"Oh, she is, all right," Val said. "All a cop has to do is walk by and she stiffens like a board. It's a gas to watch."

"And why do *you* defy the law?" was Nat's next question as he leaned forward to view the driver's face. "Tell me."

The lighter popped out and Val lifted its ringed glow while she daintily steadied his hand.

"I guess it boils down to a free interpretation of laissez faire," said the driver.

"I see. Now just for the hell of it, answer the question seriously."

"That's funny, I thought I did."

"You'd better give up," Honey suggested, exuding smoke and sweetness. "You just can't get him down to earth. God knows, I've tried."

"The law will," Nat pontificated. "It's simply a matter of time."

"Thank you, Your Honor," said Val, steering with one hand and pressing the roof with the other. "Even a little time is better than none."

"Why did you call me Your Honor?"

"Well, you sounded so much like a judge so I figured I'd sound like a prisoner."

Nat shifted his feet. The right heel jostled his camera which he then lifted from the floor and placed on his lap. His palm cupped and squeezed the upper part of his face in a way that implied weariness but was really irritation. DANGER OBSTRUCTION AHEAD loomed up and swept by as did a vivid lake in the blur of the woods. He noticed that Honey Bea was staring at him.

"You claim indifference to the penalties of the law," he said to the driver, his voice a bit gruff and businesslike. "Are you as quick to abstain from its protection?"

"What protection?" Val asked, removing the cigarette from Honey's mouth, using and returning it. "I was robbed once a couple of years ago. Came home to find the pad a shambles. Quick check and I see I'm missing a radio and some clothes. It's late, so I hop to bed and put out the light. I'm thinking about how I can get another radio. I once lent a portable job to a friend in Michigan. I decide to write him for it tomorrow. *The typewriter!* I jump up, put on the light and rummage around. My Royal is missing. So it's a radio, clothes and a typewriter. O.K., back to bed. I start thinking again. With all the clothes they took, how did they get them all out of the pad? Must have used a suitcase. *Suitcase!* I jump up and open my closet. Sure enough, my suitcase is missing. Now I'm afraid to go to bed. And that at least is there. I don't want to think anymore. I figure some soft music will calm me. Yep, the record player is gone. The records, too. Wow. I could have killed the bastards. But

I didn't report it to the police." Val looked at DeVore. "I did not report it."

Almost angrily: "Why?"

"Yeh," said Jonesy. "Hell man."

"Let him talk." Ottomeyer was caught up by the story.

"Why? Because it wouldn't have done any good. Why bother?"

"But the thief might have been caught," Victor explained, frowning as though in pain. "You might have gotten it all back. Maybe he *was* caught."

Nat agreed and Val said: "That's the myth. But I never heard of an actual *case*. Never."

"Yet there are many," said Nat.

"Well, we live in different worlds. In yours the thief is caught, the guilty punished and the victim compensated. In mine, the guilty escape, the victim suffers and the innocent hang. It balances out, I suppose. I just wish you could be a tourist in my world for a while. And I sure as hell would like to spend a day or two in yours. 'cause that's where my suitcase, clothes, radio and record player are."

Honey smiled at DeVore. "If you should see his stuff, would you let him know?"

He readied himself to reply with facts and figures and to radiate social consciousness, but it caught him again, the subtle entreaty of her perfume rising from the black cotton curves of her anatomy. And that smile, that unembarrassed look of insidious innocence simmering with sensual messages.

"There's a turn just ahead," Ottomeyer warned the driver.

"I know. I know."

"I bet the Dodgers will collapse like in '51," Jonesy was saying to Nat DeVore.

"Sorry," Ottomeyer apologized. "Didn't mean to backseat drive..."

"Baseball doesn't move me," said Nat.

"It's just that you were going so fast," Victor Ottomeyer explained.

"Were you born in this country?" Jonesy asked.

"Guess I should hand out blindfolds," Val called to Victor.

"Of course I was born in this country," Nat replied.

"Or try going a little slower," Victor replied.

"You were born here and you don't like baseball?"

"I have three speeds," said Val. "Fast, very fast and holy markerel."

"I was born in Brooklyn, vote Republican and hate baseball. So what does that make me?"

"Oh, be serious," Victor said to the driver.

"It makes you a loser," Jonesy laughed.

"You're looking at me funny," said Honey, obviously delighted.

"Oh, I'm sorry," Nat murmured, faltering slightly.

"Hope you like what you see."

Two fingers, graceful and thin, with tufts of hair between the knuckles, carefully lifted out of its socket a miniature white plastic horse's head the size of a dime and advanced it to a new socket. Someone else's same two fingers, bony and nail-bitten, converged on the black queen, lifted her, paused, and then set her down in distant country, three inches away.

Seated behind the driver, in the Buick, Eddie May studied the pocket chess set with which the two men beside him were waging a soundless skirmish. The maneuvering had no meaning for him so he searched their faces instead. Nearest was Irving Rubin, thin, nervous, with glasses, who now moved his graceful fingers to attack the dark queen with a white pawn. He struck Eddie as being intense, intelligent and Jewish. Beside him was Max Cohn, tall and balding, his dome and forehead looming as though hours of pondering had swelled his brain. Beside him, against the window of the Buick, were two maple crutches.

Eddie couldn't understand why everyone was so calm. As heavy as the sagging sky, there hung in the air a discreet sense of sin and worldly vice. Eddie, at eighteen, imagined himself sampling decadence and finding it to his taste. His college freshman blood rebelled at reliable mother-cooked meals followed by nights alone in his sex-proof bed. Capable coeds paced through the halls of NYU beyond his grasp and coolly immune to his shrewd lusting, their shyness, fear or indifference all conspiring to mock him. What he had been waiting for was a chance to free himself from the sweltering enclosure of adolescence. Today, he hoped, was a beginning in that direction. History, Psych and Trig would have to wait.

As they moved toward some secret spot in the far woods, Eddie continued studying the others. The driver, Leo Somethingorother, was large, baby-faced, silent and obdurate. Next, Ben Reno. A strange one with his rimless glasses, separated front teeth and a Bolsey camera strung conspicuously on a short strap around his thick neck. Beside him, looking expensive and shallow though oh so lovely, sat what'shername? What *was* her name? Forgotten it already. Stupid ass. Tammy or something, wasn't it? Lucky guy, Reno, to sit next to her. How does one stop staring? Her cigarette fumes curl roofward in langorous slow motion and then dart away through the slight breach of lowered window.

"Hot-rodder," said Reno, anxiously. "Where's he off to, a fire?"

"Just like him," Tanya added, "just *so* like him."

Reno turned to look at her. In fact, his attention rarely left her.

"This joker," he asked, indicating the driver in the car ahead, "what's he up to?"

"Beats me."

"You know him?"

"Some."

"Long?"

"Off and on."

"Sounds intimate."

"Can you keep like a secret?"

"Sure thing." Leaning closer, his breath pushed her back.

"He's my brother, don't you know."

"Oh, really?"

"Haven't you heard?"

"What?"

"Under this smooth stuff we're all brothers."

"You just lost me."

"That's O.K.," she said. "He just lost us."

Reno tried to spot the Mercury. It was gone.

"Yeh, what's happening? What's the rush?"

"I don't know," said Tanya. "But I'm Jewish and I'm scared."

Was she making a fool of him? Reno eyed her poker face, waiting for a sign. There was none. So he peeked for the dozenth time into the cut of her dress.

The driver emitted from his big body a thin baby's voice. "I'm not gorna chase da guy. I'm not gorna get ticketed."

"But don't lose him, huh?" Reno said anxiously.

"I'm not gorna get ticketed."

"Crazy," Tanya remarked, shaking her head. "This whole bit is simply crazy." And she threw her L&M out the window as though it were a dart.

Reno was angry. "Hot-rodder, that one up there. Are the others still behind us?"

"Still behind us," squeaked the driver.

"Hot-rodder. Wrap himself around a tree."

"Not that one," Tanya explained, sourly. "No such luck."

She pulled her dress over her knees as Reno scanned her once again. She turned away to stare at the monotonous drift of countryside. Reno pulled out a smooth pocket watch and then returned it to an inner pocket. He coughed, adjusted the rimless glasses that seemed embedded in his flesh, then he looked at her again. There was nothing surreptitious about him. The survey was rude, open and almost prodding.

"Well, we're out of the city," Reno said to her.

Brilliant, Tanya thought. It's going to be one of those days.

"Now, let the H-bomb fall," he added.

Tanya, to the side window: "Oh, that's cheerful."

"Sunday's the time to do it," he insisted. "People all outdoors and relaxed." He seemed to have thought it all out. "Sitting ducks. Whole New York area. Wham-o."

"Somehow Sunday doesn't appeal to me," said Eddie. It was as though he were trying to decide on a time for a picnic.

"How about Monday?" Tanya suggested. "Like Monday's a drag anyway."

"If I had my choice," the boy told her, "I'd pick Wednesday."

"For the H-bomb to fall? *Why?*"

"I don't know. It sort of breaks up the week."

During the quick, communal laughter, Tanya swiveled her head to smile at the boy and nod her approval. Does he shave? He looks so young. Ulysses would never have let such a youth on the trip. With Val, of course, anything goes. Eddie May, Eddie May not. A nice, clean-cut type. Dear mother would love him, the bitch. Yet Mother would have asked, "But is he ... ?" and for kicks Tanya would lie as she sometimes did when she was dating some truly Aryan type. Yes, Mother, he fills all your qualifications: he's Jewish. But how blond he is, Mother would say. So very nice and clean-looking. Tanya reached for a cigarette. Her pack was empty. Mother, why do you loathe the way I look? Why did you try to bleach my skin? Of course she's not here to answer. Oh, how terribly politely I hate her.

"Has anyone a weed?" asked Reno.

Eddie reached and gave him one. "Anyone else?"

Tanya swiveled around. The boy was looking at her. With an impish nod, she unfurled her arm to receive her gift. "Thanks, boobie."

"Light, light, who's got the light?" said Reno, palms pummeling his chest. Tanya found a matchbook from *The Forum of the Twelve Caesars.* He took it from her and lit hers first. "Korea once. Buddy of mine next to me at night. Struck a match to light my weed. Next thing I know. Wham-o. He was hit. Stretched out with the butt still in his face."

She took back the matches and said nothing.

"Don't I also get a thanks, boobie?"

"Dems who has, gets," said Tanya with a smile like stamped tin.

"Check," announced one of the chess players.

"You lost me," Reno told her.

But she had turned to the countryside again to see a woman with clothespins in her mouth fling out her arms as though cruci-fied by drudgery and toss a bedsheet over a line.

"Looks like the mean old rain has called it quits," said Eddie, hoping to draw her out.

"He's got such luck, that one," Tanya said, indicating the car up ahead and out of sight. "Nobody else would have dared start out. But he does, and sure enough the rain stops."

"You rather it rained?" the boy asked.

"No, I wouldn't rather it rained. Like I don't know what I'd rather it did. And just watch, the sun will come out, too, dammit."

Eddie made a reply, but she missed it because something small and heavy had fallen into her lap. It slid down the smooth furrow of her closed thighs and stopped at her stomach. His alien fingers quickly dug it out; Reno's pocket watch.

"Slippery bugger," he said, with his split-toothed grin. "Fell on something soft, huh? Good thing."

"You can't do that," said the chess player. "Your king's in check."

Tanya was appalled. She had witnessed a lot of sick stunts, but this was a new one. She dropped her glance East-Side style and lifted it again to Reno's face.

"So it is," said the chess player. "So it is."

"Accidents happen," Reno explained, still toying with the timepiece.

Folding her arms, she stared at the rattling rear of a Mack truck retarding traffic in its grinding climb to the top of the hill. The truck epitomized the slow, stupid pace of life itself. God, what a lousy day this is going to be, she thought. Reno was still playing with the watch, tossing it from hand to hand. The very act of sitting near him seemed to her a horror.

"So it is," mumbled the chess player, "so it is."

Reno was explaining the history of his pocket watch. In the Korean War he had been awarded several medals for bravery. But the best medal of all was this timepiece given to him in Tokyo by a lovely Japanese woman whose life he had saved from an American sailor who had gone berserk. "And don't think that's all she gave me. Generous people. Wonderful philosophy. Acceptance and what not. Wonderful country. Wonderful."

With the truck behind them at last they descended swiftly into a valley of duck farms. Tanya lowered her window to catch the wind-whipped aroma of damp grass. Life seemed filled with false clues. Val De Franco, finally out of her system, was back in her life again if only for a day. Did this have some hidden meaning? Anyway, there had been that unavoidable, predictable awkwardness when two people meet who were once close and who broke angrily. The moment becomes a composite of moments, both soft and angry, and of all the in-between times when things were almost good and still a little bad, plus the absence of that which had been so intense and all-encompassing. Now there was nothing and she felt shame. But was there nothing? If so, then why did he drive so fast? It bothered him that she did not spend last night alone. When her name goes up in lights, will that bother him, too? Her name in lights! God, she had almost forgotten. How delicious. Then why this feeling of foreboding? Was it because the man whose bed she shared did not excite her? Or that she was so deep in debt? Or turning twenty-nine and none the wiser? She was in doubt about her talent, and what was frightening was that an actress could spend so many years at her craft and still be in doubt about her talent. And then there was Val. Dear Valitchska. Still a little of him in her blood; just enough, she hoped, for immunity.

A handsome youth made handsomer in Navy whites pointed his thumb and stood statuelike as they passed, and once again Tanya sorrowed over how boyish and incomplete they were, those sacrificed in war. Also, the widening gap between herself and these youths gave her something to think about. Eddie May was too young. Val had been young too long. Would she be Eddie's first woman seen naked? She was pleased by this idea and touched. But Reno will be looking for all his worth. Well, let him. Why do such men cheapen the lovely transactions of desire? It's a game for grownups and yet they play it like children. Gimme, gimme. Such high hither and dither over a woman's bulk. All right, boys, it's only meat. Don't run riot. It's photo time and nothing else. Me? I'm doing it for the money. Stepping out of pretty clothes for the money. Well, as soon as the play opens all will be hunky-dory. The play must succeed. It must. It's got to. Like the agent says: Tanya, baby, you're gonna do great, just great. Oh, God, if we can get good reviews. Then Tanya Lando, formally Emma Kretchmar, will have come to stay. O.K., boys, here she is. Step right up. She can act. She can dance. She can sing, almost. She's a million laughs. Step right up. She walks, she talks, she crawls on her belly a-like a reptile. See her swallow flaming pride. See her escape death-defying marriage. Step up. Tanya Lando Kretchmar: her paranoia and her orchestra. Appearing nightly, nude. Yes, the play *will* succeed. It's just got to. Then no more posing ever. The first time Old Tanya posed nude she was numb. With goose pimples yet, She had come out of the dressing room too soon so that marks from her garter belt and such still showed. Faceless faces watched. Was it tough to do? No. Did it mean shame or guilt? No. It meant money. Green money. That which never once did ever fall into Old Lando's lap. Like never.

At that moment it dropped for a second time, its weight like some obscene human object pressuring itself into the furrow of her groin. Again, because it happened so fast, his hand got there first. He said: "Oh, so sorry," and was about to say something further when she turned on him in fury.

"Once more," she hissed, softly, "once more and it goes out the window. And you with it."

THE sound of rain continued in the woods after the rain had stopped. Its trickling was like a pulse growing calm after passion. At the foot of a spotted birch an impassive tapping was being made by the languid fall of water from a high leaf onto the knuckle of an exposed root, while the drenched foliage of an old oak was peppering a flat rock with isolated excitement. Hours would pass before all this would cease.

The forest overlapped the field along the shambles of a rail fence. There it held out its branches and dropped circles into a black pool formed by a tarpaulin that blanketed all of a bulky farm device except its broken rear wheel. This was at the far end of a long pasture that swept up, and then more steeply up, until it reached the Willis farmhouse where, over a hundred years ago, Old G. T. Willis, at the age of ninety-three, shot a deer through an open window while seated in bed writing his memoirs. Before he reached for his gun, he had been describing his days in the Revolutionary War and of how, under the command of General Anthony Wayne, he had helped storm the British post at Stony Point, discovering only when the shooting was over that a rifle ball had lodged in his shoulder.

The field that separated farm from forest had been used as grazing land until a year ago when most of the cattle were sold to raise some badly needed cash. The Willis place resembled none of the houses in the area, most of which looked wholesome and unfaded, as though scrubbed each dawn with a giant sponge. This particular farm, however, now owned by the Willis twins into whose hands the property had eventually come, was a mess. The inheritance of ownership began when their great-great-grandfather, Old Man G. T. Willis, finally died in his sleep after completing the one hundred and fifty-fifth chapter of his memoirs. This told how, at the age of sixty-two, he had been forced one evening into a hand-to-hand struggle, eventually knifing to death an insane Indian who had suddenly attacked him and his wife as they strolled romantically along the moon-streaked darkness of (to this day still unpaved) Tuckabunkwac Road.

It was along this very road, pocked with mud, on an inclement Sunday morning that Esra, his eye chasing a low hawk, suddenly saw them coming.

He was saddled on the porch hammock with his lengthy legs dangling over either side, his shoe tips scraping wood as the hammock stirred. Before the hawk flew, he had been worrying over a tuft of thread where a button on his cuff should have been. This had only distracted him from deeper broodings: the shabby state of the farm, the imminent release from prison of Noah his brother, the flood of debt engulfing their whole existence, the endless slavery of farm life and his total lack of talent for working the land.

All these painful issues rotated in his brain, each in turn claiming recognition for a time, until a break in his attention would briefly allow his brooding a rest.

Now the automobiles were coming up the road, though all that morning he was sure the rain had turned them back. Dismounting the hammock, Esra Willis, with one cuff loose, did something he hadn't done in one hell of a long time: he danced for joy. Actually, it wasn't a dance so much as a single dance step leading up to a proposed climactic leap over the porch railing which, he remembered just in time, was dangerously loose. He skipped down the steps instead, and then strode swiftly over the land for several yards like a man trying to hurry while hip-deep in water, until a characteristic lethargy overcame him and he settled finally into his usual drag-stroll.

Esra was peculiar-looking: no one ever denied it. Somebody once said that he resembled a man who had spent his entire life in a room with a low ceiling. He was six feet two lying down, and five feet nine standing up. It was as if he felt that height was the worst form of human ugliness. Due to his posture, his large head seemed insupportably heavy. His long arms looked idle no matter how he held them, and across a face that might have been splashed with diluted red ink and then blotted dry, there slowly spread, as he came closer, an actual smile. This, too. had not happened in one hell of a long time.

He met the four cars as they swung off Tuckabunkwac Road, parking one next to the other and close to the house, leaving mud ruts streaming behind them. Mud had caked the wheels and even splashed the fenders. The windshield of the lead Mercury had been dirtied by a rather large dropping from some passing bird. Esra's greeting was the gesture of someone brushing away a cobweb. Before a characteristic blankness reclaimed his features, his smile lived on for a few more seconds. The arrival of the cars meant he would make some money this week, after all.

Nat DeVore was the first man out. He stretched wide his patched-elbow arms and filled his city lungs with country air. Adjusting the camera strap that was pulling at his corduroy shoulder, he turned politely to give aid to Honey Bea. Needing no help, she bounced herself out of the Mercury, her black stockings kicking. Yet she accepted his sturdy arm all the same, presenting him with a fetchingly grateful smile as her eyes glowed with a ripe summer warmth. Nat, deciding to stay clear of this particular young lady, proceeded to do just that by moving ahead of the others through the open gate like a great explorer setting out into unmapped country, wondering, at the same time, why he had helped her from the car in the first place.

"Where's he at?" Esra glanced about with concern, while he continued shaking Val's hand as though it was a ritual they didn't know how to end. "Didn't he come?"

"Didn't he tell you? He *retired*. Yeh, he's out. Said to me, 'Keed, you're in command now. It's up to you.' " And Val snapped to with a smart British salute, palm forward, arm quivering.

The red blotches were altered slightly as the other frowned. Never before had they used his land without Ulysses present to give the whole thing dignity.

"Well, I'm right sorry to hear it," Esra said.

"So am I," Val replied, soberly. "Besides, I really hate these field trips."

Jonesy, flashing a many-splendored Argyle sock, climbed out to join them. Others emerged slowly, standing, stretching and moving carefully in long exaggerated steps around or over the puddles. Tanya was a pleasant sight as she wiggled into view at the door, lovely legs first, striving to keep her hemline discreetly in place and eyeing the mud that blocked her way. Deciding it was best to stand up in the doorway before trying any further move, she climbed to her feet, her figure showing to full advantage, her head higher now than the metal roof as she quickly shook a most definitely frowning no to the tooth-parted smile of Ben Reno who, after climbing out, returned to help her down. Paying no heed to her protests, he took a firm, two-handed hold of her indented waist and as she snapped, "Don't help me," he lifted her up, frown and all, and brought her down on firm ground as Jonesy, a dozen feet away, gave Harry an elbow thrust. Stifling an urge to dramatize the scene, and appearing impolite to many, Tanya walked off without a "thank you."

Strolling happily with the others, Val asked the farmer how in hell he had been. The last time they had met was about a year ago when Ulysses had needed a substitute driver. Esra, with his cuff-loose hand on Val's shoulder, mumbled "fine, just fine," while thinking that, perhaps, he should speak up after all about what his sister had whispered to him Friday night before leaving on the train for Middleton. Yet, by the time the two men reached the rise near the road that looked down into the pasture, Esra had let it all slip from his mind.

Twenty men and two young women, most of them looking oddly out of place in a rustic setting, made their way in scrambled ranks down the slippery incline to where the meadow was barely sloped at all. Surrounding them on three sides was an uncrowded forest that climbed away from them up three long hills until only the bushy tops of the trees, like hills themselves, were visible.

Tanya's heels were sinking into damp earth. She was not dressed for this kind of travel since she was still wearing her clothes from the night before. If only she had remembered to ask Val to bring his black moccasins. She was annoyed and with nobody but herself to blame.

Looking as though he could have been a student on a nature hunt, Eddie May was busy trying to remove a speck from his eye. Pulling the upper lid over the lower, and with his good eye bulging, head tilted and mouth agape, he blinked, waited, and tried again. Meanwhile, Nat DeVore (two cameras yoked around his neck, a crammed gadget bag heavy over his shoulder) fell behind every few yards to register, with infinite care and complete absorption, a new meter reading.

Only Honey seemed truly happy to be there, though she had every reason, of course, to feel otherwise. To add to her recent loss, another one threatened her as well. It was a problem too close to her and too variable for her to know quite how to handle. Among the roles she had chosen to play of late was that of lover to this energetic scarecrow whom she had met last summer by the lake. He demanded nothing, sometimes showing interest and other times not, was exciting to know and she really and truly wanted him. The vague resemblance he had to Jean-Louis Barrault, the French actor, pleased her enormously. His emaciated face, so frail and forlorn, cut deep into her soul. Yes, she wanted him. But why was he receding from her of late and what, if anything, could she do about it?

Now, walking through the open gate, tightly gripping her large leather bag, she closed her eyes, gathered up her courage, and bathed her face in the country air. Because the morning dampness had gotten into her beautiful hair, she had tied it back with a pink ribbon that fluttered like a butterfly with each step. She walked blindly for a few yards, enjoying the adventure of not knowing where her legs were leading her. Afraid to do this for too long, and aware that the ground was changing under her feet as though she were reaching the crest of a small hill, she opened her eyes to the sight of a marvelous pasture, a forest, and a funny little farm. Tension vanished: wonder and enchantment replaced it like a flood. With her head high and proud, she went forward with the others as in that film about Mormons discovering their Promised Land. At the bottom of the pasture, it was she who first noticed the miracle of the parting clouds, who first felt the sun sending its tepid breath against her indoor skin.

"Will you lookit that," she said with her head back.

"Ahhh," commented three others.

Oblivious to everything else, Nat DeVore saw the needle swing across the meter in his hand and announced, "Sun's out."

"Thank the Lord for little favors," said Ottomeyer.

"Hot damn," said Eddie May, holding his Yashica between his knees while he combed his hair.

They were all standing around in poses and postures of patient waiting. Spontaneous conversations about things photographic drew several of them into small groups. Others, having decided on *f* openings and shutter speeds, rather timidly checked their findings with a neighbor as though they were cheating on an exam. One or two walked to the nearest spread of shade to load their cameras with film.

The women meanwhile were off by themselves looking totally lost.

"What happens now?" asked Honey. "Do we just sit here or what?"

"If you want the show on the road," Tanya replied, "there's your man. Talk to him."

"Not me. *You* talk to him."

Tanya walked over and made a formal interruption. "Mr. De Franco, do you think you could arrange for us to change? The sun won't stay out forever."

"Heavens, not *mister. Val*, call me Val."

"Except that this won't help me to change."

"It would if we were alone," he volleyed, flexing his eyebrows while tapping an invisible cigar.

The farmer, nodding a series of gleeful snorts, momentarily lost another half foot in height.

"None the less…" she continued.

"None the less, I haven't answered your question. O.K., let's see. Where the hell *do* they change?" He eyed the farmer. "It's been over a year since I've done this jazz."

"Don't ask me," Esra said. "Pops always made me go back to the house."

"Did he? You're right, I remember. The old frump."

"Well, he had good reasons," the farmer explained.

"He always did," Val sneered.

"If youse really wanna make de scene, like I'll inform youse." It was Tanya again, and for a moment she was smiling. "The thing is done with blankets. You string them out across a rope kind of idea."

At this point both she and Val took a long, careful, reappraising look at each other. How gaunt he looked. How many pounds had he lost, she wondered, since they last parted? And as usual, his hair needed cutting.

To him, on the other hand, she appeared, surprisingly, the very image of herself, the exact replica of herself, and her beauty, once so much a part of his life, demanded his immediate reexamination. She was a few pounds heavier than what he once jokingly referred to her as her fighting weight. And for the occasion of their first platonic meeting she was perversely masking all her feelings. How awful it was to bump into him again was what she was probably thinking. He grew angry at her poise and reserve.

"And where the hell do you *get* blankets?" Val asked.

"You're in charge, buddy," said Tanya, sharply. "Don't you know?"

He leaned closer, his eyes bulging angrily. "Lady, I couldn't..."

"...care less," she interrupted. "Oh, boy. Too much! **Try** the trunk compartment of the Pontiac. They're probably still there from last time."

"Why'd you wait until now to tell me?"

"You're our leader, no? I thought you knew. Besides, like if I *had* mentioned it, do you know what you would have said?" Leaning closer, eyes wide, she imitated his tremor of excitement. "You would have said, quote, who the hell needs *blankets*? It's *summertime*, for crysake." Coyly she closed her teeth on a fingertip.

Val seethed but said nothing. She was brazenly the very image of what he had forgotten she could be. The others who were near them stood exiled from this private place in the pasture inhabited only by the two of them and their abrupt animosity.

"I'll get the blankets," whispered Honey.

"No, let me." And the farmer came to something like a crooked state of attention.

"Stay here," Val told both of them, and marched off. Joe Jones looked up curiously as Val passed, making his way among those standing in the field like so many trees, and he an angry hunter.

Esra's long body went into action slowly. With a great deal of wasted motion, he turned, backed up, nodded at someone, turned again, nodded at another backed off further, turned again, nodded some more, and finally, having in his opinion sufficiently excused himself, hurried after Val, who was on his way in the sunlight up